ALL ALONG THE WATCHTOWER

ALL ALONG THE WATCHTOWER

ROCK BAND FIGHTS EVIL
BOOK 8

D. J. BUTLER

WFP
WordFire Press

EBook ISBN: 978-1-68057-615-3
Trade Paperback ISBN: 978-1-68057-616-0
Library of Congress Control Number: 2023947554
Cover art by Carter Reid
Cover design by Janet McDonald
Kevin J. Anderson, Art Director
Vellum layout by CJ Anaya
Published by
WordFire Press, LLC
PO Box 1840
Monument CO 80132
Kevin J. Anderson & Rebecca Moesta, Publishers
WordFire Press eBook Edition 2023
WordFire Press Trade Paperback Edition 2023

Printed in the USA
Join our WordFire Press Readers Group for
sneak previews, updates, new projects, and giveaways.
Sign up at wordfirepress.com

CHAPTER ONE

G o to hell," Chuy said.

"Been there." Eddie Marlowe, the wire-thin, jittery rock and roll guitarist, rolled his bloodshot eyes left and right around the rubble that had once been a parking lot. The *S* on the wall above Eddie had collapsed with the brick under it, but it had left behind *EARS*, and Chuy found the combination of that word and Eddie's darting glances creepy. He felt like he was being spied on.

I think Eddie's a prophet. Maybe you ought to show some respect, ese.

No he ain't, you pinche maricón. And I wouldn't care if he was. Still, he was always looking at unseen things, Eddie.

"Done that," Eddie added.

"The Mare isn't tired." That came from Jane, who sometimes was Qayna, the stone-cold killer with knives strapped to her body and a cowboy hat.

She's not a Latina.

I didn't say she was. Shut your pie hole, idiot. I mean, shut my piehole. And don't say anything about her boobs. You ain't fooling anyone. Apparently, Jane was really old. She had crazy tattoos, seemed to crawl all over her like bugs.

1

The Mare was Jane's horse, a big black snorting monster with fangs. When Jane let the horse free to graze, it came back with bloody teeth. Occasionally, it coughed up hairballs. Just like a cat, only what came up was bits of fur and bone. Now it stood glaring at the end of the reins in Jane's hand, reeking of rotting meat. Chuy could feel Mike trying not to look at the Mare, trying to drag Chuy's hand up to grab the crosses and medals that hung on his chest. Chuy forced the hand down to his side, fixed his eyes on the big animal, and spat his contempt on the shattered asphalt on which he stood. Living with Mike in the same body was like wearing the same clothes as another person— wherever you went, you went together, and you were constantly wrestling over control. Fortunately, Mike was a pussy.

"I'm tired of the Mare," Twitch said. She was out of place among the ragged band of weirdos; she looked like a teenaged girl in skinny jeans and a T-shirt spangled with the photos of some boy band that had disintegrated along with everything else in the Fall. Dirty and scraped up, but Twitch could have been just another suburban kid.

She's no kid, check out her ... she's a fairy. Be nice to her. Chuy ignored Mike. "We can't all ride the Mare, anyway, we're tired."

"And there's gas in the truck." Eddie jerked his head at the vehicle.

"Do you hear something?" Twitch cocked her head to one side.

"There's probably cans of refried beans in the truck, too. 'Cause it's a *taco* truck. So hell no. Even if I could, which I can't."

At his own mention of *refried beans*, Chuy's shared stomach slipped momentarily from his control and growled. The truck referred to squatted in the lee of the crumbling Sears, partially concealed by an adjacent pileup of smashed Japanese sedans, all impaled like shish kebab on a single metal light pole. The truck rested in a corner of what amounted to a clearing in a forest of tall piles of junk.

The truck's red, yellow, and green color scheme offended

him. So did the strip of triangular flags wrapped around the top of the boxy vehicle, and the scratched logo on the side: *Señor Gustoso's Delicioso's* the words read beneath a cartoon of a man in a black suit and oversized sombrero offering the viewer a trio of hard-shell tacos. Chuy was a good enough speller to spot the extra apostrophe, and felt embarrassed by it.

I can do it. How bad can it be? We're tired of walking, too, Mike whined.

Shut up or I'll punch you.

We're in the same body, ese.

Chuy threw himself to the ground and started doing press-ups. He was lean from a meager diet and exertion—that, too, was partly to punish Mike, who craved candy bars almost as much as he craved booze—but Chuy had big arms. He had big arms because Mike hated press-ups. The more Mike complained, the more press-ups Chuy did.

"Ten, eleven, twelve ..."

"This is Heaven's plan?" Jane snorted, and sounded just like her horse. "I would lose faith, if I had any."

"What faith do you have to have?" Eddie asked. "Weren't you there when it all *happened?*"

"Seriously. I hear something. And it isn't seven cheerful dwarves, whistling on their way home from work." Twitch had a short walking staff, and she gripped it with both hands, like a weapon.

"Twenty-three, twenty-four ..." Chuy wasn't breathing hard. He could do press-ups all day if he had to. If he could get to Mike.

Stop this. It's ridiculous.

So ridiculous you can't stand it, you wimp. You ready to shut up about the taco truck?

I'm just saying it would be easy to hotwire the truck. Why not let me get it started?

"Faith isn't about history," Jane said. Her voice was far away, distracted. "It's the power to move closer to God. The fact that I

3

have seen the Towers of Eden and fled the ruin of Ainok has nothing to do with my confidence that Heaven can bridge the gulf between itself and its scattered, mewling creations."

"Thirty-two, thirty-three ..." Still not sweating.

Fine, I don't care. Do push-ups until the cows come home. It only makes me stronger.

You think I'm so stupid I don't know what pinche reverse psychology is, joto? More press-ups. *I can tell you'd kill for a Snickers. I can feel it.*

"Stop it," Eddie grumbled to Jane. "You're making my head hurt. So what are you doing with us, then?"

"Hi-ya, hi-ya!" Riders burst into the clearing.

There were three of them. They wore jeans and flannel shirts, and two had rifles. The third vato had a lasso in his hands and dragged it in a slow whirl around his own head.

Chuy kicked against the ground to throw himself sideways. Gunshots punched over his head, and Eddie and the others scattered left and right into the junk—Chuy lost track of them. He scrambled into a tunnel formed by a sheet of corrugated tin sagging against a pile of cracked cinder blocks, grabbing for the pistol in the back of his pants as he came up out of a crouch on the other side—

a loop of rope dropped over him, closing around his arms.

He lost his grip on the pistol, heard it *thud* to the asphalt.

You dropped the gun!

Chuy had no time to do press-ups to punish his brother, and his arms were roped to his sides to boot. He jumped, trying to drag the rider off his horse with the weight of his body.

But the rider had already looped his end of the lasso around his saddle horn, and Chuy's weight wasn't enough to budge the horse. He snapped to the end of the taut rope and bounced back as if he'd hit a wall, tumbling to the ground.

Elsewhere, Chuy heard the terrible war shrieks of the Mare, and more gunshots. The louder *booms* might be Eddie Marlowe's Remington 870, which was almost enough to comfort Chuy until he remembered that model of shotgun was as common as dirt, and anyone else might have one, too.

"Chupacabra que eres," he grunted.

The asphalt hurt. It was like being dragged on his face and belly over a cheese grater, cracked and crumbling as it was. Chuy cursed, Mike cursed inside him, and then a jagged piece of glass did Chuy an enormous favor: it cut him.

The cut wasn't big, just a short slit on Chuy's and Mike's shared right cheek, but it was deep enough that Chuy started to bleed.

Wait? he wondered. See how it turns out with the others, maybe jump back in at a key moment? Or is now the right time?

A boot kicked him in the head, grinding his cheek harder to the ground. Chuy gasped and blinked through tears of jagged pain. Forced to look left as he was, he saw something he didn't expect. It was a cage on wheels and pulled by four creatures, like a wagon a circus might use to transport a lion. But there were people huddled inside, and through the sudden blur of his impaired vision, Chuy saw men with spears poke at the prisoners, force them back away from the door. The guys were dressed like gladiators in loincloths and sandals, and looked like real dipshits. One of the guards held a machete and wore a bull-head mask, and the others took his bellowed orders. The prisoners raced around like chimps, staying in a low crouch, and it took Chuy a moment to realize why.

There was something hanging from the ceiling of the cage. Not one something, but a bunch of somethings. Somethings that looked like gigantic, man-sized bats.

Then the men with spears threw open the cage's gate and hurled Twitch inside.

Within their shared body, Mike flailed. *Go, ese! Do something!*

She's not your type.

But Chuy went.

It hurt, forcing himself out through Mike's blood. His own blood. In the moment of swimming through the thick red stream, he felt tiny, maybe even totally substanceless. He forgot, for a second, who he was. The person in the already clotting trickle might have been Mike Archuleta, bass player, drunk, and glutton. But the person who burst out on the other side, bodiless, drifting, energized, was his brother Jesus, though he'd never gone by the name his mother had given him, not since he was a tiny kid. He'd always been Chuy. Murdered, damned, bitter, Chuy Archuleta, sacrificed in his prime by gangbangers to the fallen angel Yamayol.

He wanted to help Twitch, but in the moment of his liberation from Mike's flesh Chuy saw the bull-headed vato approach. Bull-Head had blood on his curved sword and he sliced it through the air experimentally as he drew near, grunting in satisfaction at the whistling sound. The rider sat atop his horse, laughing harshly, and keeping the mount back so the lasso was tight. The boot to the head had come from the third vato, a scarecrow-like apparition with tufts of torn clothing hanging out around metal plates that had been strapped to his body as makeshift armor. He held a twisted knot of wood as a weapon; at its business end, long construction nails had been driven all the way through it and poked out as spikes from all sides.

Chuy scanned them all. None of them was bleeding. He had a nose for blood now—not a nose really, but a sense. He could *feel* blood when he was in its presence. There was blood over in the cage, but that did him no good.

The bat-things seemed to sense the blood, too. Several of them arched their leathery backs and stretched wings as if yawning. The prisoners cowered, Twitch among them. There was more blood, Chuy could feel it. But where?

"The Drays must eat," Bull-Head said. He raised his weapon.

The horse.

Chuy dove into the shallow gash on the animal's flank. Again the disorientation, he didn't know whether he should neigh or curse, and then he was shouldering aside a dumb animal spirit and grabbing the reins.

So to speak.

The vato laughing on his back pulled at the reins and the bit dug into Chuy's horse-mouth, annoying enough that the horse was unwilling to face the discomfort and let its head be pulled back.

But Chuy could take the pain.

He jumped forward.

"Whoa!" Horse Vato yanked on the reins and it hurt. It felt like dental surgery without anesthesia, a rod shoved into the tender tissues of Chuy's mouth and twisted around. He ignored it, barreled forward—

Bull-Head and Scarecrow turned. Bull-Head's face was hidden, but Scarecrow's expression was utterly priceless, for that split second before Chuy rammed his equine shoulder into the armored man and sent him spinning across the junkyard.

Neigh! Neigh! The horse inside Chuy—no, the horse spirit sharing the horse body with him—objected. It was against the creature's instincts and training to run down a man like this.

Shut up, you son of a bitch horse!

He flattened Bull-Head, catching him right in the center of his horse chest. The man went down, lost his sword.

"Whoa!" Horse Vato yelled. Chuy thought he heard the cocking of a pistol. He didn't let it slow him down. Rising up once, twice, then three times, he came down as hard as he could, plunging his front hooves into Bull-Head's chest.

Bang!

Chuy felt the bullet behind his horse's ear. It wasn't the first time he'd been killed, and he recognized the deadly blow when he felt it, bringing along with it a wall of darkness. Didn't matter. Just a damn horse.

Getting into the animal had required a push. Getting out was easy; he rode the animal's spirit out with its blood and brains, emerging again into the junkyard and whirling to watch the horse collapse.

Horse Vato threw himself off the animal, yelling.

Scarecrow turned from the pile of junk into which he'd collided and raised his spiked club. "Dammit, Bob!" he yelled at Horse Vato, and spat blood on the ground.

"It ain't me!" the horseman shouted back and pointed at Mike, who still lay on the ground, writhing uselessly against the rope. "Guy must be a sorcerer."

"Chuy!" Mike hollered.

Horse Vato and Scarecrow both stepped toward Mike with evil intent on their faces, but Chuy was in motion, too. He hurled himself into Scarecrow's mouth. Found the teeth knocked out of place and the freely flowing blood. Punched aside the startled natural inhabitant of the body and seized control.

Horse Vato cocked his revolver and pointed it at Mike's head.

And Chuy, in Scarecrow's body, whacked his spiked club into Horse Vato's grinning face. Scarecrow, it turned out, was a muscular man, and had none of the underfeeding-induced weakness Chuy felt, despite his press-ups. So when Chuy swung the club as hard as he could—the weapon's nails sank without effort into Horse Vato's face—

Chuy lost his grip—

and Horse Vato's head snapped off his shoulders. The moment of disconnect sounded like a snapping twig, and then the head and attached club winged out over the rusted hood of a blue Buick and disappeared. Chuy's momentum carried him forward so far, he tripped over Horse Vato and Bull-Head and fell to the ground.

"Twitch!" Mike gasped.

Oh yeah. Chuy climbed to his feet and armed himself: Horse Vato's pistol in one hand and Bull-Head's curved sword in the other. He advanced on the cage and two spearmen who stood outside it. Scarecrow resisted, tried to take control of himself back.

Stop it, asshole, Chuy told him.

The Bull will be angry.

The Bull is dead. I killed him.

As he stomped in Scarecrow's body toward the wheeled cage, Chuy got a good look at the animals pulling it. The *Drays*, Bull-Head had called them, unless by that he had meant the bats. They looked something like elephants, only smaller, and hairy, and they had huge lower jaws that gaped down, revealing teeth like Bowie knives.

Saber-toothed elephants?

Not that Bull. The real one.

I'm not afraid of the Bull. Chuy meant it. Dead and damned already, what was the Bull going to do to him, even if Eddie and the others were right and the Bull was one of the Fallen, the original rebels against Heaven?

The one, indeed, to whom Chuy's mortal blood had been spilt?

Who are you?

The spearmen stepped hesitantly toward Chuy. They must not know what to make of the fight they'd witnessed, Chuy knew. Too bad. He raised the pistol and fired. *Bang, bang!* Two shots to the chest dropped the first guard and *bang!* a third, right in his neck, killed the second.

MRWARUUMPH!

The Drays bellowed and shook their shoulders, but didn't burst out of the chains that held them yoked to the wagon. Chuy snatched a ring of keys off the belt of one of the spearmen and took advantage of Scarecrow's strength to pick up the dead man and hurl his corpse in front of the Drays. He didn't look at what they did with it, but the bellowing stopped and was replaced by chomping and sucking sounds.

Chuy unlocked the gate. Twitch hesitated a moment, and behind her the other prisoners hung back and watched with hollow, nervous eyes.

"Mike?" She sounded like a nervous innocent girl, but she was poised in a sideways crouch in a way that made Chuy think she was ready to kick him in the teeth if he gave the wrong answer.

"Mike?" Chuy choked. "I kill a bunch of worthless sons of bitches and risk my own neck to cut you out of jail and probably save you from instant death and you pay me back by mistaking me for *that* dumb maricón?"

"Chuy." She grinned and scooted to the edge of the cage. He helped her down.

"How about us?" The vato asking was on the tall side—scratch that, he was a giant, with huge sideburns, and he wore loose linen pants knotted with a string under a T-shirt that read *Odin's Eye Embroidery* in faded lettering. "There's an old Jewish proverb that says that if you save one man's life, it's as good as killing Goliath, because Adam was one man, and his descendant was Goliath."

"Wait …" Twitch said. "What?"

The second of the prisoners—Chuy could now see that there were three—was a shorter man, with hair shaved close to his skull and twinkling eyes. "He's not on drugs. He just talks like that."

"Killing Goliath might be easier," Chuy said. "But suit yourself."

"I'm Joe, if you need an official name," the second prisoner said.

"He likes to be called Mr. Joe," the big man added.

"Just 'mister' will do," Joe said.

"Ugh," the taller man shot back. "Just tell them you play the keyboard."

"It's more than that," Mr. Joe said. "I also play drums."

"Yeah," the big man said. "On your keyboard."

The third prisoner was a woman with long dark hair and freckles. Her black dress had a short skirt and long sleeves, and she wore a black hat that looked a bit like a battered lampshade. "I play rhythm," she said. "And lead. My name is Juliana."

"Oh hell, no," Chuy said. "Please tell me you vatos play *classical* music."

"That depends on what you mean by *classical*," the big man said.

"I don't mean Iggy Pop. Are you the singer?"

"Touché," the big fellow grunted. "I think of myself more as the *screamer*. But sure. My name is Byl, spelled B-Y-L."

"Short for Wylliam, with a Y?"

"Short for William, ordinary spelling."

"Why spell it with a Y, then?"

"Trademark reasons," Byl said. "There's a lot of Bills out there, and I wanted to stand out."

"Really?" Chuy asked.

"No." Byl laughed, then shrugged. "I just like it with a Y."

Scarecrow struggled to be free, and the fight made Chuy tired. Mike resisted, but Mike was an opponent Chuy was used to. There was something delightful about putting Mike in his place. This guy Scarecrow was just a pain.

He turned and walked back to his brother. The rock and rollers behind him called after, but he ignored them. Mike was standing now, and pulling the last of the ropes off his body. Elsewhere in the ruins Chuy heard shots, but few and far between.

The cuts on Mike's face had clotted.

"Chuy." Mike wasn't asking a question; he looked into Chuy's eyes and he *knew*.

Chuy reached up with one of Scarecrow's big hands and scratched the cuts on Mike's face with his fingernails. He ripped away the new scabs and the blood flowed again.

Chuy raised Horse Vato's pistol to his own temple.

No! Scarecrow shrieked. A wave of resistance surged up within their shared body, so fierce it almost blinded Chuy. His breath came slow and shallow, he squinted, he felt himself start to stagger and slip to one side—

Bang!

He pulled the trigger, released his grip on Scarecrow, and rushed out of the armored thug's body to rejoin his brother.

CHAPTER TWO

The rock band staggered back, astonishment on their faces. Chuy would have laughed out loud if he hadn't been snapping himself back into place in Mike's body.

"Dammit!" Byl yelled. He jumped forward to grab Scarecrow and clamped a hand over the bullet wound at his temple. "It's not that bad!"

Chuy laughed. "No, vato," he agreed. "It's much worse."

"He rescued us." The giant Byl had a tear in one eye. He laid Scarecrow down gently on the asphalt. "He was such a noble soul. I didn't realize he was so close to the edge himself."

"Ain't nobody noble in this parking lot," Chuy shot back. "Least of all *that* son of a bitch. *I* saved you, although you might not have realized it, since I was in his body at the time." He said it to baffle the musicians, and was frustrated that they seemed so … unruffled at his words.

"You can jump bodies?" Juliana asked. "Can you take any body you like? I don't suppose you play an instrument?"

"Thank you," Byl said. He dropped Scarecrow to the asphalt. "I will write a song in your honor. Or at least, yell to Juliana to play a solo."

"Uh, thanks," Chuy said. "But I only did it to save *her*," he

12

jerked a thumb at Twitch, "and I only did *that* because ..." he groped for an explanation, "because she's got nice boobs."

That's not how I think, ese.

No, maricón, but it's how you act. You're confused.

"There are worse reasons," Mr. Joe said.

"Never underestimate the power of the female form." Juliana bobbed her chin sagely.

Shut up, Chuy wanted to say, but he didn't. And then the bat grabbed him.

The blow stunned him for a moment and when he'd recovered his breath and his momentum, he was fifty feet off the ground. The bat had huge scaly legs that sprouted talons at their ends, almost like a chicken, and now that he was in its grip, Chuy saw that it had six wings. They flapped in sequence and dragged the bat through the air like a rocket.

The creature shoved rows of teeth like razor wire into Chuy's face and hissed. The fetid urine-like stink of the thing's body competed with the carrion stench of its breath and almost made Chuy faint.

Until he realized that the bat was racing for the Sears wall.

I dropped the gun! Mike shouted. *It's going to throw us against the wall!*

Shut up!

They still had the rope. The bat's talons dug into Chuy's chest and hips. He thought his ribs might be cracking and he could feel blood streaming down his brother's body, but at least Chuy's arms were free. And in one hand, he still held a length of rope that ended in a loop. Horse Vato's lariat.

Chuy felt the bat's weight shift subtly, and he knew his time was up. He snapped the loop up quickly with both hands, and because the bat held him so close, he couldn't miss. The bat drew back its long legs—

Chuy wrapped the rope around one arm and yanked—

and the bat threw him against the wall.

Three things happened in such rapid succession that Chuy

couldn't tell where one started and the next ended. He hit the wall, and it hurt. It hurt like being run over. It hurt like being cut over and over and over in Hell; Chuy had reason to know. It especially hurt in his shoulder, which felt as if it had been yanked from its socket, but because Chuy's arm was wrapped in the dangling line of the lasso, the rope slowed him down, and probably prevented him from being entirely crushed. That, and maybe Mike's leather jacket.

Second, as he slammed full-body into the big tin letter *S*, and thought for a split second he was going to lose his arm, Chuy heard a hideous shriek, a *YIIIIIAAAAOWL!* that threatened to rupture all the soft membranes in his body.

And then the bat, unable to pull up because it was roped to Chuy, crashed face-first into the giant letter *A*.

Serves the son of a bitch right, Chuy thought, too dazed to feel entirely smug, and he fell. Behind him fell all the *EARS*, one toppling letter at a time, and then the bat. Chuy landed on the hood of a pickup truck with no glass in its windshield, and bounced.

Move! Mike screamed, and Chuy, stunned but conscious, had the presence of mind to roll over and fall off the hood.

CRASH! The bat plunged through the cab and hood of the truck, crushing it. As it hit, the *E*, *A*, *R*, and *S* of the old Sears sign *karanged!* into the asphalt and wrecked car body all around, each letter collapsing into shriveled, bent tin and falling aside. The beast wasn't man-sized at all, Chuy realized, except when it was all wrapped up inside its multiple wings. It was every bit as big as the horse.

Gunshots. Screaming.

Chuy!

Chuy stood up, weaving on his feet. *Shut up, or I'll exercise.* It was a bluff. His right arm felt like he might never do press-ups again.

The bat raised its snout from the ruins of the pickup and hissed at Chuy again. It was huge, angry, and bleeding.

Chuy slipped out of Mike, who bled all over, and into the body of the beast.

Madness anger blood revenge hunger blood anger hunger blood—

Shut up, puta! Chuy bellowed.

A darkness enveloped him, chewed at him, tried to engulf and swallow him. He punched back, kicked, choked, cursed, and headbutted the shadow until it swayed back, muttering and sullen.

And beaten.

Chuy took control of the bat.

He could barely breathe. It was the rope, he remembered. He'd put a rope around the bat's neck. He couldn't see Mike very well, though he knew his brother stood directly in front of him. He saw glare, and blinding white shafts of light in all directions. But he knew Mike's odor, and smelled Mike close, and then he felt his bat-throat make a tiny, almost inaudible *chirrup* sound, and when the *chirrup* bounced back at him, he knew exactly where Mike stood.

"Chuy?" Mike asked. Chuy knew his brother was trembling. "Mierda, are you in the *monster?*"

Chuy hissed in answer and dragged himself from the wreckage. Mike dropped the rope, and Chuy carefully slipped one taloned finger (toe?) under the noose around his neck. He tugged the lasso open and shuffled backward, slipping out of the rope.

He heard screaming, and he knew it was Twitch. And with the bat's ears, he knew exactly where she was.

The bat inside him hissed and resisted. He elbowed it in the psychic face, shrugged all six shoulders at once, and leaped into the air.

He was *fast*.

Three. There were three other bat-monsters, and he could hear-sense them in a cluster together, moving east. Sonar. It was called sonar. Or echo … something. They moved toward the lake, toward downtown Chicago.

Ahead of them, at the lake's edge, his sonar sense detected something he hadn't been able to see yet from the ground. It was a giant spike. Where he thought downtown Chicago ought to be was mostly flat space—he couldn't tell from this far away if that meant low buildings, or rubble, or what, just that there weren't the skyscrapers and tall office towers he expected—but out of the plain sprouted a single nail-like tower that jabbed at the sky in challenge.

Each of the three carried a person in its talons. From the yelling, Chuy recognized Twitch. The other two, he wasn't sure. He flapped his wings, and his bat body raced after its fellows. They were weighed down with prey, and Chuy wasn't, so he quickly gained on them.

Where are you going? he asked the bat inside him. He asked out of reflex, because he was used to talking to Mike, and then almost kicked himself for trying to talk to a stupid monster.

Except the monster responded. *We serve the Bull.*

In flight, Chuy realized that he had a long tail like an iguana's. It was an important part of his balance and how he steered. But the bat's words pulled him away from thinking about the physics and structure of his borrowed body.

You security? Guards? Protect his turf?

The bat struggled, but Chuy held on. The other bats grew larger in his field of hearing.

Hunters. We bring him people.

To eat? Chuy wasn't grossed out. He'd seen weirder things than that in his life, and death, and damnation.

Hell, in a way, he'd already been offered to the Bull once himself, as a sacrifice.

We don't ask. We bring people, we are fed.

The bat was grumpy. Chuy cuffed it once again for good measure and then turned his attention to his quarry. Below and behind him, with the bat's sensitive ears, he heard an automobile engine chuckling into life.

The other captured prey were two of the rock and rollers.

Fine, Chuy had no interest in them and he could focus on Twitch. He flexed his jaw and his talons, snapped high into the air to get above the other bats, and then pulled his wings in.

He fell like a stone. His own speed astonished him, and it surprised the other bat, too, because Chuy slammed into its back with both talons splayed before it could react.

YIAWL! shrieked the bat. The other bat, the one twinned with Chuy inside a shared body, didn't resist, didn't object. On the contrary, Chuy felt a tremor of thrill shudder from the creature's spirit into his own as he jammed their shared talons into the flesh of their target's back and with a single clench snapped the other bat's spine into three pieces.

Die! Die! Die!

They fell together. In its mortal shudders, the second bat dropped Twitch, but Chuy was ready. He whipped his long iguana's tail around and snatched Twitch from midair with it, like a monkey grabbing a piece of fruit. He felt the fairy wrap her arms around his tail, and then he focused again on the shuddering monster in his claws.

He sank his teeth into its neck.

Did I do that? he wondered. Suddenly it seemed to him that the monster was in control, not him. Hot blood squirted in his mouth *hunger anger blood blood* Chuy ripped his mouth away from the wound, but couldn't resist swallowing what was already in his throat.

He hissed, in anger and satisfaction. *Blood anger hunger blood!*

And felt sick.

So sick, he almost failed to get his wings spread in time and crashed to the earth. But at the last minute he saw the vast gray slab rising to meet him, and with a resisted effort he hurled the bat-corpse from him. The dead beast exploded into a tangle of tree trunks and a bulldozer, split stem to stern as if by a giant cleaver.

Chuy shifted all six shoulders, and his wings brought him up nicely in an abrupt swoop. *Blood hunger—*

Grunting, he cut off the monster in mid-rant. He alighted on the sagging pebbled roof of a blue-and-yellow-signed Bucky's and carefully set Twitch on her feet. He quivered, felt the monster beside him snap and stretch. Chuy forced himself to shuffle backward. With his long, taloned legs, it was an awkward motion.

"Chuy?" Twitch held her fighting staff up in front of her defensively.

Chuy hissed in frustration, still tasting the metallic sludge of demonic bat blood sloshing around his bony gums. He was careful as he turned not to knock Twitch over with his tail, and then he leaped to the edge of the gas station and hurled himself into the air.

He didn't give a rat's ass about the *blood hunger blood* rock and roll trio, he told himself, and he meant it. But he had to get rid of the bat, and the logical way to do that seemed to be to attack the other bats.

He wondered what would happen when he died. He hadn't been this far from Mike since the moment Mike had come to rescue him—no, that was too generous. Mike hadn't rescued him, he lied to himself, knowing it was at least partly a lie. Mike had happened along, and Chuy had hitched a ride. But since that moment, for however many *blood hunger* weeks it had been— Chuy shook himself, trying to get rid of the beast-feeling that hung around his head—he and Mike had rarely been apart, and never far.

So what would happen to him if the bat died half a mile off the ground, and five miles from Mike Archuleta? Would Chuy find himself in Hell again? Or just wandering the earth alone and broken, like all the rest of the human race was doing these days?

He shook himself again and accelerated.

This time, the other bats turned as he approached. One wheeled away in a deceptively languid circle; its wings beat furiously, and it rocketed through the air, gaining elevation as it did. The second made a sharp U-turn, launched itself right at him—

and threw the prisoner in its claws.

Chuy's instinct was to duck, but his bat-monster copilot had other reactions. As a human being, screaming, hurtled through the air toward them, Chuy's bat body flicked its tail up and caught itself with all six wings on a draft of air, pulling slightly out of the trajectory of the human missile and plucking it from the air with its tail.

blood hunger blood hunger

Relief and sickness and a gigantic shadowy bat-presence struggled within and around Chuy, and then he had to clamp his will down hard on the monster, just one moment before he shoved the unfortunate human's head into his maw.

Chuy yanked his beast-snout back, held position with flapping wings, and looked at his catch. Juliana's dark hair was balled and disheveled under the hat she held clamped to her head with both hands, but she looked at the bat-monster holding her with a steady gaze.

"Ye gods."

The other bat crashed into Chuy and they tumbled across the sky over and over. Chuy almost lost his grip on the rock and roller, but not quite; the woman made a sound like a cat being gargled by an elephant, but she held on tight to Chuy's tail and didn't vomit.

The attacking bat got its talons around Chuy's neck. Chuy had a vision of the moment, just minutes earlier, when his own talons had snapped another bat's spine, and he trembled. With the last moments of his bat-life and an eternity of mental clarity, Chuy reached up one claw, nicked the other bat's underbelly—

felt his own neck snap—

exited the dying bat, slipped through the flowing red blood into the victor—

surprise blood hunger alarm blood—

and then Chuy elbowed aside the other bat, seized control, and snatched the rock and roller from the dead bat's talons.

He didn't care about her for her own sake. But he might need her to get back to Mike.

The dead bat fell.

With a howl of glee, the third bat plummeted from above. It fell past Chuy roaring, and dropped its prey as it went.

Chuy flapped to one side, grabbed the falling man from a midair cartwheel. It was the keyboardist who called himself Mr. Joe, and he yowled as his vertical drop abruptly became a horizontal swoop.

The diving bat snatched the dead bat with its talons a few hundred feet above the earth and tossed it to one side. The corpse crashed into the ruins of a bar that had once been called *Elmore's* and skidded to a halt in a salad bowl of rubble. The other bat fell onto it with claws extended and sank its teeth in.

blood hunger blood—

Shut up!

Chuy drifted to the earth struggling against the bat beside him. He set the two rock and rollers on a shattered stretch of sidewalk a hundred feet away and hissed softly at them in a way that was meant to simulate a whisper. He raised one muscular leg, and with a single claw he scratched a bloody X into each musician's forehead. He marked both of them just in case one ran away, but they didn't run, and they didn't resist. They just stood fixed in place and shook like trees in a rainstorm, and Chuy took off again.

The bat with him wanted to shriek a challenge, roar in delight, plunge its muzzle into a fountain of blood and meat and feast. Chuy didn't let it. Instead, he circled once to get altitude, and then fell on the feasting bat. The monster died from the sheer weight of Chuy's fall, but Chuy gripped its misshapen skull with both talons and ripped it open, just to be sure. Gore and brains spattered bat-Chuy and the blast crater that had once been a seedy little Chicago bar called *Elmore's*.

The surviving bat, the one yoked to Chuy, roared. The silent din rocked Chuy, and he clamped his will down to cut it off.

You will not kill me! the six-winged bat-monster raged.

Watch me, bitch.

Chuy rose into the air a final time. Each beat of his muscular wings was a struggle against a will that resisted his with animal ferocity, but he held on. He rose in a slow circle, trying to keep his eyes off the target he knew very well he would aim for. Suspicion flooded into his consciousness from the bat.

You cannot kill me! the bat insisted.

I killed the others, Chuy couldn't resist pointing out.

He circled above a slouching telephone pole, wires sagging but unsnapped on one side holding it up at an angle like a howitzer. Or a tank trap. The bat-demon struggled once more and then stopped.

The Bull will not like this.

Screw him. Chuy dropped from the air, all wings clamped to his sides, tail straight out behind him.

And impaled himself on the telephone pole.

The impact was so powerful it left him stunned, and too insensate to immediately notice the pain. But it also carried him thirty feet along the length and almost to the ground—his legs dangled on either side of the pole, talons almost touched the brown grass beneath, tail twitching, twitching, as the giant wooden dowel piercing the bat's chest sucked out its life.

Then Chuy was adrift on the face of the earth, in the blasted ruin of Chicago. He felt naked, weak, pulled to something he couldn't see that he knew would destroy him.

He saw the two rock and roll musicians. They squatted behind a pile of rubble, staring. They didn't see him, of course, but they stared at the dead bats. Chuy, invisible, damned Chuy, drifted across the blighted earth and slipped through his bleeding forehead into the body of Mr. Joe.

"Let's go back to my friends," he said to Juliana, straightening up.

"Friends?" she asked. "I thought I *was* your friend."

"I'm not your bandmate," Chuy said. He was tired. "Chingada madre, my name's Chuy. I was inside the horse, and the guy with the sword ..." he thought he was forgetting some links, but he was too drained to care, "and the bats. I was inside the bat that saved you, and the bat that killed itself. My name's Chuy, and I think rock and roll bands suck."

Juliana shut her gaping mouth, straightened her hair, and bowed.

"You, sir," she said, "are a badass."

CHAPTER THREE

"There's nothing wrong with playing the keyboards," Byl said to Mr. Joe.

The big man had quickly found his bandmates in the rubble.

"Now is not the time," Chuy said.

He's obsessed with this, Joe said. *Make him stop.*

"I'm just saying it's okay to say you're a keyboardist," Byl said. "There's nothing wrong with that, and it doesn't mean you have to even be good. Hell, I tell people I'm a vocalist, and what I do is *scream.*"

"Stop," Chuy said. "I'm not Joe."

"Do you play an instrument?" Juliana asked.

"No. My brother Mike plays bass. The other guys ... that's his band." Well, mostly. Chuy didn't feel any obligation to explain Crow Jane and her flesh-eating horse. "They don't have a vocalist, as it happens."

What are you doing with that band, if you don't play anything? Joe asked.

The alternative was worse, Chuy said.

As if on cue, the Señor Gustoso truck rolled into view, weaving between a wrecked Greyhound bus and a beaver dam-like structure made of telephone poles. Mike was driving.

Jane rode behind the truck and slightly to the right of it. When Mike brought the taco truck to a halt, she stopped beside it.

Eddie leaned out the shotgun window of the taco truck. "We'd give you a ride," he called to the rescued trio, "but we're going downtown, deeper into the Bull's territory." His bad eye slid abruptly sideways before wobbling back into its ordinary place. "My best guess is you want to head west to get out of the city. Out past the three-fifty-five, past Naperville, say, you'll be able to turn south more easily."

We aren't going south, Joe protested.

No one asked you.

With you in my ... what are you, in my brain? In my soul? You seem to be running the show, so if only you can hear me, I'm going to make myself heard.

How do you feel about press-ups, Joe? Chuy asked.

What?

Chuy dropped to the floor and did press-ups.

"We're going downtown," Byl said.

Eddie pointed at the nail-like spire. "That's the Bull's territory. Yamayol, one of the Fallen."

"Yeah," Juliana said. "So can we get a ride or not?"

Jane rested a hand on her hip. It was an innocuous gesture, except that Chuy knew that she had easy access to several throwing knives from that position.

Chuy got to his fifteenth press-up and stood, dusting off his hands. Joe didn't have Mike's arms, and Chuy felt winded at fifteen. "If you guys are some of the Bull's men, shouldn't you be ... attacking us or something?"

Byl laughed. "What? You rescued us."

Juliana simply gave two thumbs up.

Why would we attack you? Joe asked.

Everyone else does, chingón.

Try not being such a jerk, Joe suggested.

Try shutting your mouth, Chuy said, *or get used to press-ups.*

Why don't you call them push-ups? Joe asked. *You sound ... old. Or Canadian, or something. Are you Canadian?*

That's it. Chuy dropped to the ground and did more press-ups.

Juliana looked down at Chuy and Joe, doing press-ups, and nodded, looking impressed. "So you're saying you guys aren't here for the battle of the bands?"

Eddie frowned. "Battle of the bands?"

"The Bull needs a new band." Juliana shrugged. "To play for him when he appears on his throne, I guess. Or marches in victory parades, or whatever. Climbs the tower."

"Did he eat the old one?" Eddie snarled.

"Maybe." Juliana shrugged. "Or stepped on them, or they got killed in a battle against the People of the Serpent, or the followers of the Centaur, or whatever. But being in the band is a much better life than being some poor bastard spear-chucker."

"Better food," Byl said, "you don't have to fight as much."

"But you'd serve the Bull," Eddie said.

"In the most harmless possible way." Byl nodded. "I'm not saying it wouldn't be a compromise with a corrupt system. But life is full of hard choices."

"And the choice I want to make is the one in which I stay alive," Juliana said.

Eddie harrumphed, but he didn't disagree. His eye slid sideways again, and he shuddered, almost imperceptibly.

"Unless, of course," Byl said, "you guys are making a better offer."

"Dammit," Eddie growled, but then he rapped the side of the truck with his knuckles. A side door opened; Twitch stood inside, beckoning the trio in with one hand.

"That's what I'm talking about!" Juliana bounded up into the truck and Byl followed. The big punk had to lean forward to climb inside and then sat on the floor of the truck. Chuy followed last, savoring the burn in his borrowed arms and the sullen silence of Mr. Joe.

Why "Mr. Joe," anyway? he asked.

The kids called me that at the planetarium. It seemed a little more rock and roll than just plain "Joe." Like, I don't know, Joe is a guy you see down at the bar. Mr. Joe has secrets and might kick your ass if you're not careful.

Chuy snorted.

Plus, then I can make the joke about just call me mister.

The grill and frying vats and refrigerators had been ripped out of the back of the taco truck, leaving a big empty space without seats or seat belts. A long sheet metal window ran along each side of the truck, with a track and support struts that allowed it to be propped open. Chuy, Juliana, Byl, and Twitch sat, and Mike put the truck into gear.

Chuy could hear the hoofbeats of the Mare through the truck wall.

Eddie swiveled in his seat to face the others. "We're going to steal something from the Bull." He looked Byl and Juliana each in the eye, his own eyes staying in a stable position. "It will be crazy dangerous, but if we succeed … we can probably get away.

And maybe even use what we steal to make a safe place for … for humans. For you."

"Probably?" Juliana said.

"Well, that sounds as good as our odds with the battle of the bands," Byl said. "Remember, we don't even know if Yamayol listens to screamo."

"Not to mention the fact that we don't actually have instruments," Juliana added.

"I'm confident we could loot something between here and downtown," Byl said. "Chicago has a long history of looting. They feel warmly about it."

"We leave no one behind." Eddie's voice was firm.

"Yes, we do." Twitch's voice cracked. "Only just the dead."

Eddie sighed, his shoulders bowing.

"I guess if I'm dead, I won't care," Byl said. "What are we stealing?"

"You'll care," Chuy said.

"A flag," Eddie told the big singer.

Byl frowned.

"Oh," Juliana said. "You mean *the* flag."

"You've seen it?" Fierce light flashed in Eddie's eyes.

Juliana shook her head. "Heard about it. It's magic, or something. People follow the Bull because he has the magic flag. People hear him from far away, and his words touch their hearts, because he's carrying this old flag. Used to belong to the pharaoh, or something like that."

"To the kings of Judah," Eddie said. "It's how David gathered his men in his bandit days, and how the wealth of the world flowed to Solomon. It's called the Ensign to the Nations, and God first gave it to Noah."

"I don't remember that from church," Juliana said. "Mind you, it's been a while."

"Yeah." Mike didn't turn around. He drove beneath a stretch of elevated highway, between shattered warehouses. "We're sort of the *untold* part of all the Sunday School stories."

"Noah needed the power to summon the whole world," Eddie explained. "Everyone had to be given the opportunity to repent, or it wouldn't have been fair to drown them in the flood."

"I'm not sure the Old Testament God is most noted for being fair," Byl said. "When I read it, he just seemed really angry."

"Humanity will do that to you," Eddie said. "But God gave Noah the Ensign, which allowed him to gather the people together for their last chance. And some of the stories say that the only ones who repented were three women, who married Noah's three sons, then got on the ark and sealed the doors just as the rain started to fall."

"What about the animals?" Juliana asked.

"Noah had animals on the ark," Eddie said.

"Right, I did my time in the Bible Belt." Juliana's smile was almost condescending and almost annoyed. "I mean, did the Ensign allow Noah to command the animals? And I've read some of those old, weird stories, so I've read that Solomon built the temple using the services of djinn—construction genies. I thought it was because he had a magic ring or something, but now I'm wondering if maybe it was the magic flag."

"The Ensign," Eddie said.

"Okay. The magic flag called the Ensign." Juliana smiled again.

Eddie shrugged. "Maybe. But at some point, the Ensign got taken away from the kings of Judah. Apparently, Josiah thought he had it when he rode out to Mount Megiddo, and that it would summon all kinds of allies to his side, or turn his enemies in his favor. Neither of those things happened, and instead he got shot with an arrow and died."

"Wait," Byl said. "I never did the Sunday School thing, but, uh, did you just tell us a story about how the Ensign stopped working? So why do you want to steal it?"

Eddie ground his teeth.

"We're pretty sure the real Ensign never stopped working," Twitch said. "We think someone hid the real thing from Josiah, some old faithful priest or mischievous fairy or someone, and Josiah had a useless dummy. A fake."

"A fairy." Juliana chuckled.

Eddie glanced briefly over his shoulder at the road.

"And how do you know that Yamayol has the real one?" Byl asked. "I mean, he's successful, sure, people follow him, but maybe he just has charisma. Maybe he's a good leader. I mean, a little authoritarian, I'll give you that, but maybe people are choosing to follow him. Maybe he offers good health benefits."

"Well, I have heard stories about a flag," Juliana reminded him.

Byl nodded.

"We just know," Eddie said. "We have sources."

Supernatural sources, Joe said.

Chuy felt tired. *I don't know what's supernatural anymore, man. But Eddie has had visions for years. Used to be, they were all visions of hell and loss. Recently, he started seeing more hopeful things.*

Why's that?

You like press-ups that much, do you?

Yeah. I'm okay with getting stronger.

Mr. Joe wasn't a whiner like Mike, at least. *I guess Eddie's a prophet. After centuries of nothing, Heaven chose a prophet for our times.*

Weird prophet.

Weird times. Chuy shook off a feeling he didn't enjoy, because it was too much like gratitude. He was glad Weird-Eye Eddie had come down into Hell, bringing Chuy's repressed brother Mike, and that Mike, in some misguided attempt to make up for getting Chuy killed, had carried Chuy piggyback with him out of Hell and back into the United States of America.

Or at least, what had been the US of A. Somehow, in their absence, the whole thing had collapsed.

"This all sounds fine to me," Juliana said. "Or anyway, it's no weirder than anything else that has happened in the last six months."

Eddie looked over his shoulder at the road again. "Left at the next light."

"The next *working* light?" Mike asked.

"No, just … there. Left *there,*" Eddie said.

"I guess you're a Chicago native," Byl said. "So are you taking us by some shortcut down to the Tower?"

"The Sears Tower?" Mike asked.

"That's what it used to be," Juliana said. "I guess maybe the old Sears Tower is still somewhere inside there, like the skeleton inside a giant, but the Bull and his people have been building on the Tower since he got here. You've seen it. You can't help but see it, from twenty miles away."

"From fifty miles away," Eddie muttered. "Yeah, we saw the Tower, and yeah, we'll end up there at some point. That's where the Ensign is."

"Are we going looting for musical instruments?" Byl asked. "A mic and a PA would be good. I don't know how much crowd noise I'm going to have to scream over."

We're not looking for instruments, Joe said. *This is something personal to Eddie, there.*

Chuy found himself frowning with Joe's face. *How do you know? Can you see his spirit or something, ese?*

"Ese" is much better than "chingón." No, just look at his face. He's feeling something really intense, now. Shame, maybe. And fear.

"We're going to rescue my family," Eddie said.

How much was the damned, queer-eyed, rock and roll prophet going to tell these people he'd just met?

"They're in Chicago, but the Bull doesn't have them?" Juliana asked.

"I think they're in Chicago," Eddie said. "I think I know someone who can help me find them." His voice and his eyes both dropped. "And I think it's safe for me to go to them."

Heavy, Joe said. *Is he cursed?*

I'm not sure I like your running commentary ... chingón.

Are you saying I'm guessing wrong, ese?

No, I ... I'm saying you're smarter than Mike. Look, Eddie sold his soul to the devil, but he got ripped off.

Everyone does.

Yeah, I guess that's what they teach you on the first day of your Deals with the Devil class. And Eddie's curse, look, it's complicated, but one part of it is he's been seeing the death of his family for years.

Not anymore? Joe asked.

Not since the angel came. And seeing as the angel told us to get the Ensign to the Nations, along with other things, and Eddie's from Chicago, we made a beeline right here.

You know, bees don't actually fly straight.

Chuy dropped to the rattling metal floor of the truck and started press-ups again.

Are you cursed, too? Joe asked. *You know, I can talk while you're doing push-ups, this doesn't actually bother me.*

Chuy grunted in irritation and quit, throwing himself against the side of the truck. Realizing that everyone else was staring at him, he growled.

I'm not cursed, he told Joe. *I'm dead.*

Your brother is the driver?

Yeah. And he's the pinche chingón who killed me.

"Okay," Juliana said, "I have missing family, too. I'm in."

Byl nodded. "We all are."

"And the keyboard player?" Eddie asked.

Chuy stepped aside, letting Joe have control of his mouth again. "Yeah," Joe said. "Let's do the right thing."

"See?" Byl said. "He just called you a keyboard player, and you didn't even get mad at him."

Just for fun, Chuy didn't let Joe answer.

"Right here," Eddie said to Mike. "We're going to that apartment block up there."

Byl raised his head. He was so tall, he just needed to stretch a bit, and he could peer over the dashboard from where he sat. "I'm not going to say that block looks nice." he said. "It looks like a crappy tenement, and if I lived there I'd be doing my best to move out, as soon as I could. But it isn't smashed flat or burned, like everything else is. You sure that's not protected by Yamayol?"

"It might be," Eddie said grimly. "But I'm guessing it's just protected by Missy Broussard."

"Oh, good," Byl said. "When I woke up this morning, what I was really hoping was that I would get in a fight today with a girl named Missy."

Mike pulled the taco truck to a stop on a wave of shattered asphalt punctuated with splintered gas pumps. The pavilion that had once protected the pumps from the rain hung down at an angle like a lean-to; the tiny gas station itself, once a brick building scarcely bigger than a kiosk, was a scorched ruin.

"Missy is an old woman." Eddie climbed out of the car and the others followed him. Crow Jane sat astride her razor-toothed Mare; the big beast wasn't even breathing hard, and it grinned maliciously at Chuy. "Mike, you stay with the truck. Jane, you're the only wizard we got."

"You think you'll need me inside?"

Eddie shook his head. "This was a rough town before a fallen angel took over. Mike's good in a fight, but Twitch is still … is still figuring out how to fight in her new body. I was hoping you'd defend the truck, and cover our retreat, if we need it."

New body? Joe asked. When Chuy said nothing, he pressed, *Come on, humor me.*

She's a pinche fairy, Chuy said. *Or maybe she was a fairy, and now she's been reduced to a human being. She used to be able to shapechange and fly, and now …*

Jane nodded. "Where are you heading?"

Eddie pointed. "Basement apartment, there at the corner of the building."

Jane drew her pistol—the one that made people insane, and could kill monsters—and settled into a waiting position.

Eddie removed a duffle bag from the front of the truck. He opened it on the asphalt, revealing a small arsenal of firearms and other weapons. "We have an assortment, ladies and gentlemen. What do you like to shoot?"

I'm more of a scientific instruments kind of guy, Joe said.

Too bad. Chuy selected an automatic rifle, two magazines that went with it, and a box of ammo.

Juliana armed herself with a pair of pistols. Byl took a Bowie knife, a blued steel wheelgun along with a handful of bullets, and a long, squared, two-handed club.

"What's that thing?" Mike asked.

"I think they call it a tetsubo," Eddie said.

"Good to know," Byl said. "I would have just called it a club."

"Who is this woman we're going to visit, anyway?" Juliana asked.

"She's the witch who sent me to the crossroads," Eddie said. "Where I sold my soul to the devil and started this whole mess."

"Oh," Byl said, "good."

CHAPTER FOUR

S he'll have defenses," Eddie said, pumping his shotgun to chamber a round.

Eddie led, and Chuy followed at his shoulder, rifle ready. Mike was taller than Eddie, so Chuy was used to thinking of Eddie as short. Joe was about Eddie's same height, so Chuy couldn't see over the guitar player and had to drift farther to the right to have a line of sight in front of him.

"Obviously, she has some kind of defenses," Juliana said. "These buildings are still standing. I can even see glass in most of the windows."

They headed toward a cracked-asphalt-and-red-brick funnel that bored between two of the tenement buildings. Beyond, in the darkening shadows of evening, Chuy saw a glint of metal in an open space. Was that a cage?

"Like, tough guys with guns defenses?" Byl asked. "Or like, flaming demons with whips for tails defenses?"

"Could be either," Eddie said. "Could be both."

"I'm ready." Juliana walked with both pistols pointed at the ground ten feet in front of her, as if preparing to step onto the set of a Hong Kong gun fu movie.

As they rounded into the mouth of the alley, Chuy saw three men standing at the other end. They wore patches of leather and corrugated metal strapped to their bodies, as if they had distributed a biker's riding gear among them for armor and made up for the missing parts by sawing up a length of irrigation pipe. The two on the sides held spears made of sharpened lengths of rebar lashed to the end of eight-foot poles; the one in the middle had empty hands, and a revolver sagging at a wide, red vinyl belt.

Not men. Youths. Kids who should be in high school.

Or maybe the witch will be defended by the cast of Lord of the Flies, Joe quipped.

Don't joke about flies, Chuy said. *Pinche flies will mess you up, chingón.*

In hindsight, we could have scouted this out better.

"I'm looking for Missy Broussard," Eddie said. "If it helps, I have candy."

The youth in the center spat on the asphalt. "Not that interested in candy, to tell you the truth."

"No?" Eddie continued walking, as if he planned to simply stroll past the three. "Is Missy still in the bottom corner, son?"

"My name's Matthew," the young man said. He was black; lean and narrow-shouldered, but he had a broad face and tight, curly hair. He spoke with just a hint of a Jamaican accent.

"Okay, Matthew," Eddie said. "And your friends here?"

"Mark and Luke. Really, Marco, but he goes by Mark."

Eddie grunted. "Figures. I take it Missy still lives here?"

"To tell you the truth," Matthew said, "I'm much more interested to know if you have whiskey or cigarettes."

The other two young men raised their spears and pointed them at Eddie's chest. "Or crack," Mark said. He was muscular and thickly tattooed with markers indicating that he had once belonged to a major gang with roots in Mexico.

Chuy was pretty sure the gang didn't exist anymore.

"Or gasoline," Luke said. He was the tallest of the three,

white and sunburned, and he seemed to lean forward onto his tiptoes as he made eye contact with Byl.

"You kids should be playing too many videogames and trying to figure out which girls on the block are up for a little midnight macking," Eddie said. "The world got too grown up for you, too fast, and I feel bad about that. Still, it ain't really my problem. You're going to want to get out of the way right now, or I tell the big guy with the tetsubo to let you have it."

"What's a tetsubo?" Matthew asked.

"It's a ninja club," Mark said. "It's what that big mohawked son of a bitch is carrying."

"No ninja could carry a weapon this big," Byl objected. "You can't sneak around in a castle carrying a two-handed club. Even strapped to your back, it would get in the way when you tried to hide or climb. There's a reason ninjas fight with throwing stars and tiger claws and really short swords. The tetsubo is more of a samurai weapon."

"The samurai used swords," Luke said. "A long sword called a katana and a short sword called a wakizashi. Pretty sure a samurai with any honor at all would avoid the tetsubo like the plague."

"So, what?" Mark asked. "It's a weapon for peasant foot soldiers?"

"Don't knock peasant foot soldiers," Juliana said. "That's who is always left standing in the end."

"I'm not a samurai anyway," Byl said. "And I'm perfectly happy to call it a club."

"Puta, we're being held up by a bunch of pinche karate nerds," Chuy said, "and it turns out that we're karate nerds, too."

"Look," Eddie said, "forget about the club. Have you noticed that the rest of us have guns? Don't make us fight you."

"Do you belong to the Bull?" Matthew asked. "If you belong to the Bull, we ain't letting you pass, irregardless."

"Yeah," Luke said. "Tell us about the Bull of his mother."

"Irregardless isn't a word," Chuy found himself saying, and he realized that, in his distraction, he'd let Joe take control of his mouth.

"If you understood what I meant," the boy said, "then it must be a word. And don't think we aren't capable of stopping you. There's more to us than meets the eye."

Eddie waved a hand to cut off the argument. "We're not with the Bull."

"How do we know?" Mark asked.

Eddie raised his voice. "Missy!" he barked. "You must be listening." He paused, and his voice echoed around the inside of the apartment complex. "This is Eddie Marlowe, Missy. I'm not saying you owe me, but ... it's time to do the right thing!"

The armed boys bristled, edging forward with their spears, their leader resting his hand on the butt of his pistol.

Get ready to rock, Chuy said. *If I leave you, can you shoot this thing?*

Aim for the center of mass, Joe said. *I'm not crazy about shooting at kids.*

What about shooting at gangsters who are shooting at you first?

I can appreciate the nuance.

"What is the right thing, then, Eddie Marlowe?" a new voice called.

Chuy kept his attention on the boys, but he was aware of a woman behind the three toughs with evangelists' names. She was old, dry and thin, but her posture was perfectly erect. Her skin was such a deep brown it was almost black, but her hair and her eyes were white.

"I need help, Missy!" There was a crack in Eddie's voice.

"You fled here once!" she called back. "You told me that you saw visions of your family's deaths, and that in those scenes, you were present. You told me that the only way to protect your family was to be gone!"

"I know what I did!" Eddie yelled.

"I know what I did, too! I helped a man whose career was

going nowhere by giving him exactly what he asked. You wanted to meet the Man at the Crossroads, and I connected you."

"You did." Eddie's voice dropped and he hung his head.

"And I even warned you to be careful, didn't I? To beware the codicils, to read all the fine print?"

"You did," Eddie murmured.

"And you screwed up anyway." Missy clicked her tongue and shook her head.

"Oh," Matthew said, "you're *that* guy."

"You're kind of a legend around here," Luke said.

"People think maybe it was you that brought the apocalypse," Mark added.

"I'm that guy," Eddie admitted. "But I didn't bring on the apocalypse. That was Jim's fault."

The old woman walked forward into the alley. Chuy realized that night had overtaken them, and the only light that crossed the alley came from a couple of windows back in the apartment complex. Missy Broussard wore a dress like a spiderweb, which seemed to hang from her shoulders but also sometimes seemed to bunch around her like a ball. She had mismatched flip-flops, one pink and one green.

"What do you want from me, Eddie?" she asked.

"I came back to find Sharon and the girls," he said. "Things have changed."

"They think you're dead," she said. "Claimed on the life insurance and everything."

"That turns out to be the only good investment I ever made," Eddie muttered. "Is Sharon with someone?"

"I don't know. They don't live here."

Eddie frowned. "You threw them out?"

"They left." The witch gestured at the brick walls around and behind her. "Not everyone sees this as enough of a kingdom."

"But you could find them if you wanted to," Eddie said.

"Child," she said, "I could find *anyone,* if I wanted to."

"Help me find Sharon," he said. "Help me make it right."

The old woman hesitated, then nodded. "Let them in, boys."

The three young men stepped aside. They gave Eddie a wide berth, a light of new respect shining in their faces.

Passing out the back end of the alley, Chuy looked around. But for the absence of electric light, in the interior of this complex, you might not know that civilization had fallen. A dozen people stood on walkways and leaned out windows to watch them. The metallic glint came from a sprawling jungle gym in the courtyard. At its center was a metal spider with a wide smile and dinner-plate eyes, squatting over rubber squares bolted to the ground; other towers, slides, climbing walls, bridges, and sliding poles had clearly been dragged in more recently and sat unbolted on the cracked asphalt.

Missy Broussard led them down a single flight of iron steps into a room stacked high with bundled newspapers, tied with twine, and comic books that were not tied together. She tapped one stack of the garishly colored booklets with a knuckle as she passed and laughed. "If I had whiskey, I might have to pass it out to the boys. But I don't, so I pass these around instead, and they do the trick."

"They're just kids," Chuy muttered.

"They are who I have," Missy Broussard said, "but no, they're not just kids."

Missy passed a silent, dusty boiler and pushed open a metal door. Beyond, orange light flickered. Chuy smelled rust, dust, and rat droppings.

"Should we post a guard here?" Chuy murmured. He didn't trust the place, didn't trust the kids with spears or the staring eyes in the courtyard.

"No." Eddie took a deep breath. "Come in with me, no need to post a watch outside."

What's Eddie afraid of? Joe asked.

Ugh, you again? Just when I'd finally forgotten you.

Sorry to spoil your fun. Doesn't Eddie seem nervous to you?

Yeah, cabrón, he does. Do you think he shouldn't be?

Joe chuckled. *Depends on what's behind that door.*

Chuy gripped the rifle tighter for reassurance and forced himself to follow closely at Eddie's heels.

Behind the metal door was a single room. Judging from the smell, there was a chamber pot that Chuy couldn't immediately see. A cot lay wedged into one corner, and in the center of the floor squatted a broad, wooden table, with one thickly uphol-stered wooden chair on the far side, facing the door, and six slatted wooden folding seats. A kerosene lamp burned low on the center of the table, squatting over a dark tablecloth covered with astral signs.

Missy Broussard shuffled around to the upholstered seat and eased herself into it.

"You can lay the guns aside," she suggested.

Eddie nodded and disarmed himself. Chuy followed his example, laying the rifle on the floor and then lowering himself into one of the folding chairs. Byl and Juliana did the same, setting down tetsubo and pistols, though Eddie noticed that when Byl sat, he eased the Bowie knife into his lap.

Did the old woman wink at the big fellow with the mohawk?

From beneath the table, the witch produced a tall black hat and passed it to Eddie. "Hold this a moment."

Eddie took the hat in his hands.

Chuy smelled grease.

Is that hat full of chicken bones? Joe asked.

"Tell me about Sharon," she said.

"Sharon's my wife." Eddie's voice cracked again, and a tear ran down his cheek. "She deserved better than me, but I never tried to do her wrong. I never cheated on her, never disrespected her. The only time I lied to her was about going down to the crossroads."

"Do you feel drawn to her?" Broussard asked.

"She's half of me." Eddie slumped in the chair. "I'm not a man without her."

"What will you do if you find her?"

"Get her to safety," Eddie said. "Protect her."

"And if she's dead? If she and the girls are both dead?"

Eddie sobbed. "I don't know. Finish bearing the burden laid upon me, and then ... and then I guess I'd have no reason to live."

The old woman nodded and took back the hat.

"Ask your questions."

"Is Sharon alive?" Eddie asked.

The old woman peered into the hat. "She lives. Your daughters live. They're together."

Eddie smiled. "Are they in Chicago?"

The witch chuckled. "Chicago does not exist anymore." She peered into the hat. "Your family is within the former bounds of the city that was once Chicago."

"Everybody's gotta be a lawyer," Chuy muttered.

"They're downtown," she added.

"That doesn't sound good," Byl said.

"Shhh," Juliana hushed him.

"Are they free?" Eddie asked.

The witch looked down into the hat and shook her head. "They're slaves of the Bull."

What kind of slaves? Joe asked.

You really think that matters, ese?

Some of the Bull's slaves are more like employees. Some are food, waiting to be plated up. Believe me, it matters.

"Where are they kept?" Eddie continued.

"They are in his retinue. They serve him by day and are chained in his palace at night."

Eddie shrank back from the witch and her hat. His odd eye was going crazy, leaping repeatedly to the side and then back to center again.

"What are *you* seeing?" the witch asked.

"Her death," Eddie groaned. "It's a vision I thought I had shaken off. I see her ... them, dying in a palace on fire. I am there." He dropped his face into his hands. "I was wrong. I can't save them."

The witch placed her face down in the top hat, shutting out all light. She remained there, hunched over the hat and perfectly still, for a minute, or maybe more. When she lifted her face again, her eyes were dark, pitted hollows in the lamplight.

"You can't save them at the palace," the witch said. Her voice sounded old, dry, heavy. "But they will be at the tower for the concerts."

"Concerts?"

"The battle of the bands," Juliana said.

"Yes," Byl hissed. He gripped the hilt of the knife as if he intended to stab someone with it then and there.

"You can find them there," the witch said. "I do not foresee their deaths."

"That will do." Eddie stood.

"I didn't say that I foresee no deaths," the old woman said.

"I'm a grown man," Eddie said. "I learned years ago that death is always in the cards. Can I save my family?"

"Yes."

"Will it cost my life?" he pressed.

"There will be a cost."

"Can we still recover the Ensign to the Nations if we rescue my family?"

The witch frowned. "The Ensign to the Nations?"

"The Bull's banner," Byl said.

"The magic flag," Juliana added.

The old woman looked back into the hat. "Yes," she said. "The flag will be there. The Ensign."

Eddie picked up his shotgun. "You know what happens next."

"I do," she said.

"But you haven't tried to stop me."

"I deserve the vengeance you plan to mete out."

"It isn't revenge," Eddie said. "What you offer ... what you led me to ... people shouldn't be able to do that."

"And my people?" she asked. "The people in these apartments? Who will protect them?"

"I will call them to a better place," Eddie said.

This doesn't sound like it's going in a good direction, Joe said. *What better place?*

Hell if I know, Chuy said. *I'm not even sure what I'm doing here, except that I think it's the least worst place I could be.*

The witch nodded, stood, and flung the hat at Eddie.

Eddie was already raising his shotgun and squeezing the trigger.

Boom! Boom!

The gun flashed bright in the small concrete room and left Chuy deafened. Eddie fired early, so the first shot took the witch through the legs, also cutting through the bottom half of a suddenly shrieking flock of chickens that hurtled at the guitar player. The second shot struck the witch squarely in the chest, flinging her back against the wall and then dropping her to the floor.

Chickens swarmed over Eddie, scratching him and bawling.

Chuy batted fowl away from his own face. He smelled blood as everyone in the room took scratches to the face and arms from the birds.

Then, outside, he heard screaming.

CHAPTER FIVE

Juliana got out the door first; she was faster than Byl and Chuy, and Eddie was bogged down in the swarm of fowl. Chuy was right behind her, though, scooping the rifle off the floor and charging past the boiler and then the comic books.

He hit the top of the iron stairs right at Juliana's shoulder and turned toward the sound of the screaming, which came from the alleyway by which they'd entered the apartment complex. The white kid, Luke, was in the grip of a four-armed, crimson-skinned, scaly creature. Tufts of hair stood out like wire bushes at irregular spots around the monster's body, and it had a goat-like face, with the teeth of a ravening wolf.

What are those things? Joe asked.

Chuy had seen them in Hell, but he had seen many things in Hell, and for most of them he had no name. He raised the rifle to his shoulder and fired a short burst.

Matthew and Mark charged the monster, Mark with his spear and Matthew firing his pistol.

Why had Chuy picked the rifle? Pistols, or a submachine gun, were so much more in line with his experience.

He had picked it because Joe had objected to weapons generally, so Chuy had picked the biggest weapon in the pile, to show that pinche planetarium vato who was boss.

Maybe that hadn't been the wisest response, or the most mature.

The monster he was shooting at was big; Chuy aimed at its chest and he hit it. It shuddered and bled, staggering back a step, but it didn't die. And then it raised Luke over its head in all four arms.

Matthew and Mark flung themselves forward. In the darkness, Chuy saw a glint on Mark's shoulders, and for a moment he thought the young man was wearing body armor. Then Mark dropped his forelegs to the asphalt.

His forelegs …

Mark sprang up to attack the red, scaly monster in a beetle-like shape.

The giant Byl reached the courtyard, dragging Eddie with him. Both men bled from multiple scratches, and Eddie seemed to be having trouble focusing. He sagged in Byl's grip and pulled away, but Byl was stronger and didn't loosen his hold.

"Demons versus demons," Byl said, watching as two beetleoid men dragged one red monster to the group, prying open its claws to free their friend as other red beasts pummeled their black carapaces. "It's a kaiju fight, playground sized."

"What's up with Eddie?" Chuy asked.

"He's acting a little weird," Byl said. "I think maybe he's allergic to chickens or something. Who's the second in command?"

"*Second* in command?" Chuy snorted. "There's not even a *first* in command. This is a rock band."

"Oh, right," Byl said. "I knew there was a reason I liked you guys."

Bam! Bam! Bam!

Juliana's pistols flashed; one of the red scaly demons had broken free from the beetles—three big, black insects now fought a red wall of muscle—and raced toward the rock and rollers.

Chuy raised the rifle into position and fired a short burst ... then a second ... then unloaded the magazine entirely, spitting fire into the demon's torso as it raced toward him, slowing down, stumbling, and then finally collapsing to the asphalt in a puddle of black blood.

For good measure, Byl raised the tetsubo one-handed and brought it down hard on the monster's goat-like head.

"I'm not in charge, ese," Chuy said, "but I don't think we can go out that way."

They backed away from the fight, looking for another exit. People swarmed down from the apartments, armed with fire axes, poles, knives, makeshift spears, and clubs. The wall of human muscle poured itself, thrashing and stabbing, into the bottleneck where the demons and the beetles fought, and pushed.

It might be enough to push the demons back, but Chuy had no intention of finding out.

At the edge of the witch's building, an alley ran out to the street. This alley had been closed off with a sheet of steel twelve feet high; in the shadow, Chuy could still see the welding sutures where the sheet had been melded together of small scraps. A United Waste sticker on one piece suggested that the wall's creators had torn apart and reassembled a couple of dumpsters to make their barrier. Barbed wire ran in loops across the top.

"Blocked," Chuy muttered, and turned to look for another exit. Maybe they could climb over the roof of one of the buildings.

"Nuh-uh." Byl pulled the shotgun from Eddie's unresisting hands and took aim at the spot where the steel wall and a brick wall were bolted together. *Boom! Boom! Boom!*

"Oh, the subtlety." Juliana pressed herself against the edge of the brick to watch their backs, pistols ready.

Byl fired until the shotgun was empty, then handed it back to Eddie and marched forward with the tetsubo. A half dozen swings was all it took, and he had battered the steel and brick joint apart, folding back the steel like origami and opening a passageway. Chuy had to put one hand on the steel and one hand on brick and push himself up and into the opening, but he was able to vault through. Byl handed Eddie over, then he and Juliana crossed.

Tires squealed and Chuy started, bringing up the rifle—

But the arriving vehicle was Señor Gustoso, and Twitch threw open the side door, shouting for everyone to pile in. Behind the truck, Crow Jane's Mare rose up into a statue-like pose, the immortal rider wheeling and pointing her pistol down the street behind the taco truck. Cavalry were rushing toward her, men wrapped in steel with long, rusting spikes poking forward from their shoulders and their foreheads and the chests of their horses. The beasts foamed at the lips and screamed hostile, hawklike cries.

Yanking up the hand brake, Mike was shoving something small and green into his ears.

Ear plugs.

"Get in!" Chuy pushed Juliana, nearly getting shot for his efforts, then leaped into the truck himself. Byl unloaded Eddie into Twitch's arms and then turned to face the oncoming riders, tetsubo raised in both hands.

The riders drew nearer. They raised rusted lances.

"Now!" Crow Jane shouted.

Twitch slammed shut the door of the van and Mike cranked the radio. A bumping, growling blues-rock-gospel song so monotonal it might have crawled directly out of a bayou cranked from the speakers.

Let me tell you a story
A shack of sugar and bone
Two little kids in the forest
They're cold, they're tired, they're hungry, they're alone.

Chuy could barely hear the pop of Jane's gun, which meant that Joe could barely hear it. Barely, though, was enough to make the keyboard player lose his grip on reality—along with Twitch and Juliana, who screamed simultaneously and began punching and clawing at each other, and at Eddie and Joe.

Crow Jane's gun was as legendary as her steed; every shot brought madness.

Chuy felt the punches that Joe took to the face and gut, and Twitch's hands around Joe's throat. He didn't see or hear whatever insane visions pushed the others to violence. Mike slammed the truck into gear and launched forward.

For some reason, Eddie didn't react. He took the blows and lay on the floor of the truck. What had really happened to him back there in the witch's basement?

Byl. Byl was outside, and would have heard Qayna's gun without mediation, and would be experiencing madness.

Joe's flesh had been torn open by the witch's chickens, and he was still bleeding. It was easy to slip through the openings on the torrent of blood, and Chuy exited the van.

The cavalry had fallen mostly upon itself. Chuy saw horses and riders impaled together, men trampled under hoof, and men slashing and stabbing at each other still. He saw Jane firing calmly, emptying her old-fashioned pistol into the warriors as a thin line struggled still to charge her. With each shot, the air around Chuy seemed to compress and then thin out again, as if the bullets were affecting reality, or time.

Byl roared, sidestepping a charging rider and then swinging the tetsubo. The big son of a bitch was so tall, he clubbed the rider right in his face. The man's headgear, a football helmet with a razor crest bolted onto the top, popped right off, and the head came with it. Head and helmet separated as they flew, arcing out back over the following warriors.

Byl roared and chased the horse, striking the headless body again, between the shoulders.

Then he turned and saw Qayna, just as she fired her last shot.

No! Chuy roared, but of course, Byl couldn't hear him.

Byl raised the club and charged Qayna.

Her eyes cold, the rider grabbed a knife strapped to her forearm.

Chuy briefly wondered what he was doing as he dove toward the giant with the mohawk. He owed this man nothing, and, since Qayna was also a sorceress, there was a chance that his interfering might get him truly destroyed.

He didn't have an answer.

Byl was still bleeding from the chickens' attack, too. The wounds gaped like open doorways in his massive flesh, and Chuy slid into the highway of the man's blood and took control.

First, the knife.

Chuy threw himself sideways. The sudden shift into Byl's perspective was disorienting, because Chuy was higher off the ground than he was accustomed to, so Chuy accidentally leaped the wrong way ... toward two unseated riders, one wielding a spear and the other gripping something that looked like a scythe fashioned from a lawnmower blade and a heavy dowel. He hit the ground hard.

But Jane's knife missed.

"I've got control, bruja!" Chuy shouted. "It's me, Chuy, in the big guy!"

Damn you, let me go! Byl raged. *By Odin, I will tear you limb from limb!*

The only limbs I have are yours, ese.

The spearman reached Chuy first and kicked him in the belly, flipping him over onto his back. At some point, Byl had lost his grip on the tetsubo, and Chuy floundered, trying to find it.

The man with the scythe leaped forward, raising the scythe above and behind him and screaming something incoherent. He was aiming for Byl's head. He brought the scythe down—

and a knife handle appeared in his throat.

He fell on top of Chuy, who managed to grab the pole of the scythe. The body smelled like sweat and bratwurst and he landed hard, knocking the wind from Chuy's borrowed lungs.

Jane had her back turned—someone was charging her from a different direction.

The spearman returned, charging at Chuy with his weapon tucked under his arm, spearpoint held low.

Chuy couldn't get the scythe into play properly. He was holding it by the blade end, and there was a dead body lying across him. The spearman roared.

Chuy extended Byl's long arms, gripping the blade and pointing the butt end of the scythe's pole at his attacker's face—

they collided. The spear sank into Byl's shoulder. The butt of the scythe's handle crunched into the other man's face, grinding his nose flat with the force of his own charge. The attacker groaned in pain and fell sideways; he dragged the spear with him, and his weight levered the dead body up and off of Byl, yanking the spear's tip from Byl's flesh.

Dammit, that hurts! Byl roared.

Can you see straight yet? Chuy asked.

He spotted the tetsubo. Throwing the scythe aside, he picked up the war club. Fifty feet from him, the Mare kicked to keep two men with swords at bay, while Jane threw knives at them. A third man, holding a pole with a lasso on the end of it, crept up behind the horse and rider.

Is the sky supposed to be orange? Byl asked.

Chuy charged. Swinging the club overhead, he conked the pole-lasso fighter directly on the top of his head. The man's plastic helmet shattered and his skull went with it; he hit the ground without dignity, a dead sack of meat.

Chuy liked having Byl's reach and muscle. *What are you, a stevedore or something?*

I'm an embroiderer. The sky's still orange. The sky's orange and I'm talking to myself.

That's … unexpected.

I owned an embroidery shop before it all hit the fan. We made patches, caps, that kind of thing. Are you real?

I'm real, ese. A real ghost, believe it or not. You're such a big bastard, I expected, I dunno, that you were in a biker gang or something.

I danced in a few mosh pits when I was young. Screamed in a few punk bands, too. There's better money in baseball caps.

There used to be better money, Chuy said, and felt a little sad.

Yeah. The sky. It's blue again.

Jane wheeled the Mare around. The wave of cavalrymen was destroyed, dead and ground into the asphalt. She swung easily down from the horse and plucked knives from dead bodies.

"Are you sane?" she asked.

"Byl is recovering," Chuy said. "In the meantime, this is Chuy, I'm in control."

"The Horn doesn't break your mind?" The Calamity Horn was Jane's pistol, which she had had enchanted in an effort to kill herself, but which instead caused madness in those who heard its report, and apparently could also kill the Fallen. Eddie had told Chuy and the others about seeing Jane shoot Semyaz dead at the Infernal Council.

Also, apparently, the gun had caused World War I.

"I guess not." Chuy shrugged.

"I'll hold onto that information for future reference." Jane sprang back into the saddle. The Mare grinned at Chuy, showing bloodstained fangs that looked like they belonged in a wolf's maw. "Are you coming?"

Chuy looked down the street along which the van had disappeared. "Don't see how I can catch up on foot. Guess I'll have to leave Byl." He felt reluctant.

Hey, Byl said.

Jane extended a hand. "We leave no one behind."

"Yeah." Chuy thought of that moment in Hell when his brother had suddenly appeared. He had taken Mike for just one more torturing apparition, at first, but then Mike had offered to carry him out.

Chuy had said yes because it gave him an opportunity to needle Mike.

Why, really, had Mike offered in the first place?

"Byl's pretty heavy," he said. "Are you sure?"

Hey, Byl said again. *I can hear you. Hell, you're talking bad about me with my own mouth.*

"We leave no one behind. Eddie taught me that."

Chuy took Jane's hand. She was surprisingly strong, hoisting Byl's body onto the horse's back though he was four times her size. The Mare made not a single noise of complaint or adjustment of posture, no indication that she had even noticed Byl's mounting.

"I think he might have learned that in the Marines," Chuy said. "That wasn't really the ethos of my gang."

"I never even had a gang." Jane turned the Mare's head with the reins and spurred the beast into a quick trot. "Until now."

The Mare lowered her nose to the ground as she ran.

"Can she smell the truck?" Chuy asked. "I mean, I know it used to be a taco truck, but it didn't seem especially … odorous … to me."

"The Mare can track anything by smell. I've seen her follow an arrow by its scent before."

"Now I *know* you're talking bullshit."

"Am I?"

The trail they followed took them downtown, toward the spike of a tower that rose near the shore of Lake Michigan. "Why is it always towers?" Chuy muttered. "Why does every city want to claim it has the tallest?"

"That's an old impulse," Jane said. "Take it from someone who was around to see the very earliest of cities. The tower is the staircase that ascends to Heaven, so the tallest tower is the most heavenly … or, in this case, the best siege ramp. The city supports the tower and is the sign of the tower's might."

"Here I thought Chicago was built on the cattle market, or something."

"Cities have markets. They also have cathedrals, which is another, very old, form of the tower."

"What do you mean by siege ramps?"

"Where do you think this is all going?" Jane asked. "What do you think we're doing?"

"Following Eddie's crazy visions, I guess," Chuy said. "So most likely, it's all going nowhere."

"But if Eddie's visions are right, then Heaven is under siege, by Hell, organizing its own power alongside the starving, angry masses of Earth. And if Eddie's burden is a true one, then our quest is to bring Earth into the battle on the side of Heaven."

Their path led from city streets, up an on-ramp, and onto a raised highway. Ahead, brake lights seemed to indicate that the taco truck had come to a halt.

"How do we do that?" Chuy asked.

"I think we have to build a tower," she said. "And probably a city."

"I hate to say anything surprising," Chuy said, "but there's not a single architect in that taco truck."

"We'll need the Ensign to the Nations," Jane said. "And the Arm of the Lord."

"I thought those were weapons," Chuy said.

"Of course. What do you think we're talking about?"

They approached the truck. The door slid open and Juliana, Joe, and Twitch tumbled out.

Look left, Byl said. *Pretty sure that's it.*

Chuy looked left and saw a tall hotel. The Hilton sign on the roof was no longer illuminated, but it was visible in the glow of bonfires and burning buildings that flickered up from the street. Through the windows, on all stories, Chuy could make out lights —again, illumination cast by fires and lanterns, rather than electric bulbs.

It's a Hilton, he said. *What about it?*

That's where we're going. That's where all the bands are.

CHAPTER SIX

M ike and Eddie stepped from the vehicle. Eddie carried his shotgun slung over his shoulder, and Mike checked the magazines on a pair of pistols.

"We leave the truck here." Eddie sounded tired, or distant.

"You feeling okay?" Chuy asked.

Eddie grinned and shook his head. "Hell, yes. Chicago has mostly collapsed or burned to the ground, and what's left is run by a giant, bull-headed fallen angel, who has my family enslaved. And our plan for dealing with this situation is to impersonate a rock and roll band."

"We *are* a rock and roll band," Mike said. "Don't knock the rest of us just because you suck."

"Give Eddie a break," Twitch said. "Timing isn't everything."

"But if you don't have timing," Mike said, "a strong sense of pitch would be nice."

"Listen to you, chingón!" Chuy laughed out loud. "Someone woke Mikey up!"

Eddie chuckled and shook his head.

Chuy couldn't get away from the feeling that something was wrong.

"I'm glad to hear your standards are low," Joe said.

Juliana sniffed.

"We need instruments and we need to be in the battle of the bands," Eddie said. "I think the easiest way to get both those things is to steal them."

"From someone else who is hoping for their big shot," Mike pointed out.

"True," Eddie said. "So let's try to pick some real assholes who don't deserve a shot."

"I have a feeling that won't be a problem." Chuy gestured at the hotel, which stood fifty feet away from the elevated section of highway. "But how do we get into the hotel?"

"That one is no problem at all," Jane said. "Hold tight."

Chuy barely had time to wrap his arms around the rider before the Mare sprang into full gallop. He pressed his borrowed face against the shoulder of her long coat and closed his eyes. His stomach turned from sheer speed.

Can I get off now? Byl asked.

Chuy responded by clamping down tight on his control of the big guy.

The Mare turned, hit the edge of the highway, and jumped.

Chuy tried to breathe while the animal sailed through the air, but he couldn't. The night felt cold on his skin and his breath was a stagnant miasma in his lungs that wouldn't stir. Beneath him, in entirely too much detail, he saw men with knives and spears, and a couple of rifles spread among them to boot, walking a patrol circuit through the yard and parking lot of the hotel.

And then the Mare landed, sailing through the blown-out external wall and clattering to a halt on shredded carpet and concrete.

"Now we can get off," Chuy said. He rolled and fell to the floor with a painful thud.

Holy shit. Byl laughed in Chuy's head. *Is she going to ferry us across one at a time?*

It was a good question. "Now what?" Chuy asked.

"You stand guard here," Jane told him. "I'll worry about the others."

Chuy gripped the tetsubo with both hands and reconnoitered the hotel hallway. He found no light and no occupants. The elevator doors were shut and the floor indicator was dark. Opening the door into the stairwell, he listened and heard voices above and below.

Voices, including raucous music and singing.

Qayna had chosen an unoccupied floor by which to enter the hotel.

In the meantime, she had located a fire hose, tied it to a heavy bedframe within one of the bedrooms, and dragged the bedframe snug against the door. Holding the end of the hose, with the length of it heaped up in the hallway, she rode the Mare back the way she'd come, galloping down the hallway and then leaping over the gap to the concrete and the taco truck.

While Jane made the far end of the hose tight on the truck, Chuy checked her knot at this end. He'd never been a Boy Scout or a sailor, so he was no great expert, but the knot was tight and wasn't slipping, even when Mike backed the truck up slightly to take out the slack.

They'd turned a fire hose into a tightrope.

Then Chuy posted himself in the hallway, flat against the wall, with his back to the open air. He kept one eye on the truck and one on the stairwell.

The gang came across the tightrope crawling, hands gripping the fire hose and knees slung over it. Eddie came first, then Mike, then Juliana. Twitch walked over the hose as if over a bridge— maybe to show that, broken fairy that she was, she still had poise and agility. Then Qayna leaped back across on her horse, with Joe on behind.

"Hey," Joe said, meeting Chuy's gaze with indignant eyes, "she offered. I'd be a fool to say no."

"I wasn't saying anything," Chuy said. "Hell, she lugged me across, and I'm in this giant. Three times your size."

Twice at most, Byl objected. *Come on.*

"The great thing about you being in … inside Byl," Joe said, "is that he can't rag me about being a keyboard player."

"But *I* can," Juliana said. "It's okay to be a keyboard player. No shame, bro."

Joe growled.

"Temporary respite, anyway, Mr. Joe," Chuy said. "Sooner or later, I'll be in another body."

"Do you feel disoriented, changing bodies like that?" Juliana asked.

"I'm getting used to it."

"Do some of them feel more right to you?" she continued.

"Uh … yeah, I guess. It felt pretty weird to be inside that pinche giant bat." Though if pressed, Chuy would have had to admit he preferred being inside the bat-demon to being trapped in Hell.

That didn't make him grateful. Mike owed him. Mike would always owe him.

The guitarist nodded.

"How do we pick a band to …?" Mike asked.

"The floors above and below this one both have lights," Eddie said. "We go floor by floor, until we find a situation we like."

"A situation we like being some poor pinche bastards we can rob," Chuy said. "Just so we're clear, and no one gets on any moral high horses."

Eddie nodded.

"I don't know," Qayna said. "We're trying to save the world. I think that gives us moral superiority over some crackhead quartet that is just auditioning for a better job in post-apocalyptic Chicago."

"Are you trying to save the puta world?" Chuy asked. "Or are you trying to die?"

She cleared her throat. "No moral high horses."

Following Eddie's voiceless lead, they ascended to the floor above. Juliana and Joe pressed forward right behind Eddie, but Mike and Twitch drifted toward the back of the gang, with Chuy. As Eddie and Juliana knocked on a door, Mike leaned in to whisper to Twitch, within Chuy's earshot.

"Does Eddie seem okay to you guys?"

"No," Chuy said, "he does not."

Twitch snorted. "He's tired. He has the burden of command. And now, after years of not seeing his family, he's come back to rescue them, with the knowledge that he might be mistaken about his changing visions and he might very easily bring his family death rather than salvation."

"I get all that," Mike said. "But he's suddenly talking less. He reminds me of Jim."

"Maybe he's sick," Chuy suggested.

"Jim turned on us at the end," Mike reminded them. "All that time on the road, and him being the strong silent type and fencing like one of the three musketeers, and then when it came right down to it, he chose his girlfriend over us. Adrian died, Twitch was shattered, and Jim broke up the band."

"I am not shattered," Twitch said. "I am … fixed."

"You mean repaired?" Chuy asked.

"I mean frozen," the fairy explained. "Fixed in one shape. Immobilized."

Who is this person? Byl asked.

Twitch was a fairy, Chuy said. *She got broken in Hell.*

"Like a bug," Mike said. "Stuck to a piece of Styrofoam with a pin."

"What's your point?" Twitch asked.

"My point is that I think something's wrong," Mike said. "I would be pretty sad if that meant that Eddie was about to turn on us."

"Choose his family over the gang?" Chuy felt heat on the skin of his borrowed face. "That would be really shitty, wouldn't it, Mike? Everyone knows the pinche gang is always more important than family."

Mike's face fell. "Chuy, mierda, I'm sorry."

"I'm not going to let you *stop* being sorry, either. Chingada madre. Don't think I wouldn't jump over there and make you do press-ups in a heartbeat, if I felt like it."

"Well, this is an unconventional conversation," Joe said.

Rat-tat-tat-tat-tat! Gunfire sounded from down the hall. Eddie and Juliana started shooting back through an open door into a room shedding yellow lamplight.

"Hey, rhythm section!" Juliana called.

Boom! A louder blast, maybe a shotgun, punched a hole through the wall near Eddie's head. Qayna spurred her horse, leaped right over Eddie, and crashed through the door.

Chuy and the others rushed to catch up.

More shooting erupted from the room under siege, forcing Eddie to press himself flat against the wall and inch away from the opening. Joe squinted, paced sideways from the door, and then fired a tight circle of shots right through the wall into the room.

The shooting stopped.

Chuy followed the rest of the band into the suite. Within, Qayna had dismounted and the Mare grazed on a bloody mess in the corner; by the look of it, the mess had once been human. Joe and Juliana and Eddie rummaged through a room that looked as if a hurricane had hit it.

"You could have shot someone," Juliana said reproachfully to Joe.

"I *did* shoot someone," Joe said. He pointed to a dead blond man in a leather halter top and skirt who lay slumped against the bar in the corner of the room, clutching an automatic rifle. "Pretty sure it was that guy. Three or four times, by the look of it."

"Just decided to start shooting, huh?" Chuy asked Eddie.

Eddie looked at his combat boots.

Juliana shook her head. "We knocked. They started shooting."

"Pretty sure they were high," Joe added.

"And maybe involved in a gang war," Juliana added. "That one kept yelling 'Dirty Rounder' at me."

Chuy sighed. "Well, what did we get for instruments?"

Twitch emerged from one of the bedrooms. "The good news is, this was not a polka band."

"Why is that good news?" Joe asked. "I can play the accordion. Any chance they played zydeco?"

"The good news for you," the fairy continued, "is that there's a keyboard. Also half a dozen guitars, a couple of basses, a drum kit. These guys were sitting on a lot of musical instruments."

"Maybe they weren't a band at all," Chuy mused. "Maybe we just robbed the local gear store."

"Probably not, though." Twitch grinned. "Most of the instrument cases and a couple of the drums have a name painted on them. The Flamers."

"We're the Flamers now," Chuy said. "Not the worst band name."

"Eddie and the Flamers would be even better," Juliana said.

"You don't name the band after the pinche rhythm guitar player." Chuy snorted.

"No?" Juliana smiled innocently. "People thought Echo and the Bunnymen were named after a drum machine. Except that wasn't even true, there was no Echo. But if you think Chuy and the Flamers is better—"

"'Eddie' is fine," Chuy said.

"What *do* you play, Chuy?" Twitch asked.

"The vibra-slap," Chuy said, "and the washboard."

"How about the harmonica?" the fairy suggested. "There's a box of harmonicas."

"I don't play the harmonica," Chuy said.

"They have the key stamped right on them," Mike said. "I can tell you what key we're in and you can just blow random notes."

"I would suck."

"First of all," Twitch said, "you will suck just like half the rock and roll harmonica players who ever tried and failed to bend a note. And second, remember, we don't need to *win* this battle of the bands. We just want to get close enough to grab Eddie's family, and get the Ensign to the Nations."

"Principally, the Ensign to the Nations," Qayna said.

Eddie stared at his feet.

"You are all forgetting something really important here," Chuy said, "and that is that I don't have to play an instrument at all. I can ride along passively inside Byl here, or whoever, or just hang out with you while you play."

"Right," Eddie muttered.

"Is that everyone with an instrument?" Twitch asked.

"I will play drums," Qayna said. "I have a lot of years of experience, and, no offense, Twitch, but you have no rhythm."

"I think of myself as a jazz drummer."

"Think of yourself as the tambourine and bongos and slide whistle player."

"Slide whistle?" Chuy laughed. "Did we knock over a rock band, or a nursery?"

"And the horse?" Joe asked. "It's a great horse, don't get me wrong, but unless it can dance or solve math problems on stage, it's going to look a little out of place."

Qayna removed her pistol holster and all her knife sheaths from her body, one by one, stowing them all, weapons inside, carefully in the Mare's saddlebags. Then she whispered something into the horse's ear, stood back, and whistled.

The horse trotted out of the hotel suite and disappeared.

"Just like that?" Chuy asked.

"The Mare is no ordinary horse," Qayna said.

"Pretty sure it's not a horse at all," Joe suggested. "Some horse cousin-species, otherwise extinct. Or a horse-bear hybrid. Horses eat grass."

"The Mare is the last of the horses of Diomedes," Qayna said, the lines of her mouth flat. "She'll come when I call."

Joe raised his eyebrows.

"I'd say we could go ask other bands how this process is supposed to work," Juliana said, "only last time we knocked on a door, the band shot at us."

"The stakes are high," Eddie mumbled. "Chuy, can you go scout out the situation below for us?"

"You don't mean in this big hulking Viking body, do you? Or half-Viking, half-bear hybrid?"

Thank you, Byl said. *I'll take that as a compliment.*

"I was thinking the other way," Eddie suggested.

"Okay," Chuy agreed. "But one of you needs to be bleeding when I get back. I'm not saying I prefer it to be Mike, but, you know, if one of you *wants* to rough him up a little, it won't hurt my feelings."

"Huevos," Mike muttered.

Chuy took Byl's Bowie knife and made a small incision in the back of the giant's forearm. Flowing out of the body with the blood, he left the band to sort musical instruments, look for string winders and tuners, and reload their weapons, and drifted down the elevator shaft. He couldn't fly, exactly, but he fell slowly, so once he was through the crack between the elevator doors, he just let himself drop.

Near the bottom of the shaft, he caught himself on a ladder rung, slipped back into the interior halls of the hotel, and looked around. In the ground floor lobby, he saw bands lined up in sullen clumps, waiting to be loaded onto school buses that idled beyond the shattered glass of the lobby doors. Men in spiked armor lined the musicians up and grunted at them, poking with maces and gesturing menacingly with spears.

None of the musicians carried weapons.

More men in spiked armor plodded up the stairs. Chuy raced to get ahead of them, wishing the elevator worked, and finally pulling beyond the first of the men two floors below where his bandmates were.

Rushing finally back into the gunfire-chewed suite, he found that Byl's wound was bandaged. Juliana stood holding her own hand; a small cut on the palm bled, and she twisted the flesh to keep the blood flowing.

Okay, then. Chuy entered the guitar player via her blood. Grabbing control of her vocal cords, he warned the others: "No guns."

"What do you mean?" Byl looked up from a hard-shell travel case of dynamic microphones. "Wait, are you Chuy?"

"You got a minute or two, tops," Chuy said, "and a guy in armor is going to get here to escort you down to the lobby. You'll have to bring your musical kit with you."

"But no weapons," Eddie said.

"Not unless you can hide them," Chuy told the guitar player. "I didn't have time to exhaustively search anyone, but I saw a long line of bands, and none of them carried anything so obvious as a shotgun or an AK-47."

Qayna raised her hands. "Unarmed."

The others quickly looked at their musical gear, hoping maybe to find secret compartments for storing guns. Eddie and Mike, in the end, both slid knives under the linings of their stolen guitar cases.

"We'll have to do this by wit alone," Eddie said, and Chuy realized what had been bothering him so much. Eddie's eye had stopped moving. It was still, a normal, healthy-looking eye, and not the ducking and diving orb that marked Eddie's visions and made him seem shifty at the same time.

"Wit." Twitch laughed. "Too bad we don't have any!"

There was a knock at the door. "Flamers?" a voice asked.

CHAPTER SEVEN

S o, Juliana said. *Tell me how you feel.*
   What's that supposed to mean? I feel fine. Hell, I barely feel
anything at all. I'm a pinche ghost, if you hadn't figured it out.

Ghosts feel, Juliana said, *or they wouldn't be ghosts. You're pissed*
at Mike, which means you can't really acknowledge that you're also
grateful to him.

I'm not grateful to him. That little chingadero got me killed. Gang
required a sacrifice, and he was supposed to go get a rival gang member,
but he chickened out. Chickened out, and he was pissed at me for what-
ever damn thing, so he threw me under the bus. Under the torture and
sacrifice bus, if I'm not being clear enough. Which is how we got here.
Did I mention, irony of ironies, that I was sacrificed to the Bull himself,
Yamayol, the monster who now runs this town?

Yeah, but we also got here by Mike picking you up in Hell and
carrying you out.

Kinda seems like the bare minimum he could do, don't you think?

Yeah. Except that who else ever does that?

Chuy growled.

He sat pressed against the window of a school bus, a dark
cherry Gretsch Electromatic on his lap, arms wrapped around

the neck. Byl squeezed onto the other end of his seat, spilling out into the aisle and onto the seat across the aisle. Joe sat on Byl's other side, and Jane, Eddie, Mike, and Twitch sat behind them, in the last row of the bus.

"We're the biggest ensemble," Mike muttered.

"Good," Twitch said. "If we get into a fist fight, remember, these are not your instruments, and it's okay to hit people with them."

"It was okay to hit people with our own instruments, too," Mike said. "As I recall."

The instruments crowded the band's laps, which meant that Jane's drum kit was very spare, just a snare and a kick drum.

So, do you feel any different? Juliana pressed.

Like what, did I suddenly forgive my dumb asshole brother, because you pointed out that he did in fact carry me out of Hell? No.

No, I mean, being in a woman's body.

I guess I look cuter. Is that what you're looking for? Look, after a million years without a body, just getting tortured by my own past in Hell, I guess I'm not really focused on the details.

Not a million.

No, not really a million. Seemed like it, though. You're shorter than Byl, so that's an improvement.

Well, I'm glad I'm prettier than the ogre.

"I didn't say you were prettier than the ogre, I just said you were smaller." Then Chuy realized that he had spoken out loud.

"What ogre?" Byl asked.

Thanks.

"We're here," Qayna said.

The bus rolled to a stop in a parking lot jammed thick with other buses, and the musicians were dragged out by armored men. Being at the back of the bus, the band had a moment to look out the windows and get their bearings.

The tower rose directly above them. Close enough to examine it in detail now, Chuy saw that what appeared from far away as a needle, up close looked like a needle and thread. A spire shot straight up from a concrete pad; he couldn't even see how big around the base of the spire was, but it might be a mile, or maybe more. The spire was built of buildings, ripped from their foundations and deposited here, and cars and trucks, and boats, and even large trees, all welded closely together without apparent thought to structural integrity or aesthetics. If the Sears Tower was inside there somewhere, it was thoroughly hidden now.

Eyeballing the spire, Chuy thought he could see paths by which one could move through the inside of the needle, hopping from building to building and climbing through automobiles.

But there was another road, spiraling around the outside of the needle. It was constructed of highway, roads that had been uprooted and laid here, resting on steel girders and cables and stone columns that radiated out from the spire. The whole thing looked like a spiral staircase of junk, or the demented vision of some beatnik junkie of the ragged, wasting DNA of the modern world.

On the ribbon road, one loop off the ground, a stage had been built of timbers and shingled slabs of wood. It faced upward, and a band was just finishing its set. They performed with their backs to the crowded lot full of buses, and facing up toward a spectator box.

The box was embedded in the body of the spire, and might have been ripped out of a baseball stadium. Multiple rows of wooden bleachers left and right flanked a central pair of enormous seats on which sat a huge man, perhaps thirty feet tall, with a bull's head and hooves, and a similarly enormous woman with the head and wings of an eagle. The bleachers crawled with winged, serpentine, scaly things of various descriptions, but the space immediately around the central seats held humans—they trimmed and polished the hooves and talons of the two Fallen in the center, and oiled their skin, and carried tidbits of food to the giants' mouths.

Surrounding the lot of buses and the spire on all sides, a crowd stretched down to Lake Michigan, visible a mile away, and into the distance on all other sides. They roared, sang, and danced to the music.

"There." Eddie's voice sounded strained, and he pointed straight up.

Above the Bull's head, several loops around the spiral highway, a standard-bearer held a flag. The bearer looked like a man made of wax who had been exposed too long to flame; his flesh dripped and was striated with black streaks, and he rode a metal-wrapped caterpillar with a slack jaw and a heavily fanged, open mouth. The standard-bearer held in one hand a long pole that reached forward and drooped down; hanging from the end of the pole was a green bough. The banner dipped and bounced slightly, in time with the music, as the band onstage finished its final chorus.

"I would really feel more comfortable if we had guns," Mike said. "Lots of guns."

"That is the Ensign to the Nations," Eddie said.

"The branch?" Chuy asked.

Eddie nodded. "And the pole, I guess."

"Is there a plan?" Twitch asked. "I used to feel that plans were too confining, but then, I used to be able to show pony."

Show pony? Juliana asked.

You got me, Chuy said. *Some kind of fairy thing. I think she's also able to turn into a bird.*

"Here's ... the plan," Eddie said. His voice jerked, but his eyes were steady.

What was wrong with Eddie Marlowe?

The others watched the guitar player, nodding slightly. The band on the stage finished; the vast audience rumbled, a noncommittal sound that might have been approval or might have been simply notice. The singer, a tall waif whose height was exaggerated by two feet of completely erect purple hair, pumped his fists toward the crowd and then turned to face the Bull.

The Bull pulled slightly away from his female companion. "Next," he rumbled, his voice rolling like thunder down along the ramp and across the crowd.

"We're your band!" the purple-coiffed singer screamed. He raised both hands over his head, throwing horns on both fists. "The Bull of his mother is great in the morning! Great in the morning!"

Yamayol leaned forward out of his throne-box, snorting. Chuy thought he could feel the heat of the Bull's breath hundreds of feet away. "No," he growled. "You are not. You are not great in the morning. You are not the Bull of his mother. And you are not my band."

Then he swiped with one fist. It was a casual gesture, but he struck the singer and knocked him from the stage. The singer sailed like a purple-headed comet, over the crowd and the waiting rock bands, and crashed down on top of a school bus, still. A faint mist of blood rose from the impact site and settled on the bus, painting the orange a deeper shade of red.

The bands shuffled forward. Chuy found himself at the bottom of the ramp.

"The plan?" he asked.

"You can … get back your … pistol, right?" Eddie asked Qayna.

"Yes," she said.

"Then the plan is … that you shoot Yamayol," Eddie said. "Don't kill him … just wound him. That's the distraction."

"These minions will pursue me," Jane said.

"You'll live." Eddie grinned, a forced, spasmodic smile.

She nodded.

"So Jane runs away?" Mike said. "And the rest of us go running up the ramp and take the Ensign? I guess that makes sense."

Eddie grunted and nodded.

"When do we go?" Chuy asked.

Eddie blocked out the sun with one hand and looked up at the Bull. "Now is good."

Jane put two fingers in her mouth and whistled. The tones were shrill and long, in a descending cadence, and then she hooked both her thumbs in her belt and waited.

"Soon?" Eddie asked.

She nodded.

The band had earplugs; they'd found them along with tuners and picks and string winders in the hotel room, and now they put them in.

"Right," Byl said, stuffing his ears. "I remember going crazy last time. I didn't hate it, per se, but I can only give it three out of ten. Maybe four. Can't dance to it. Not something I need to repeat."

"I don't understand," Joe said.

"The gun makes people crazy," Mike said.

"How crazy?" Joe asked.

"Well, the first time it got fired, it started World War One."

Joe put in his ear plugs.

The next band climbed onto the stage; they didn't last through an entire song. They played some kind of fusion rock, with a polka-style accordion driving underneath and two guitars with wild, shimmering flange on the top. As their first song, a Doors cover, came to a halt, the Bull screamed at them without words. They staggered away, falling from the stage. Some died on hitting the asphalt beneath, but at least two of them managed to climb to their feet and lurch into the surrounding crowd.

Joe eyed the accordion but held his position.

Chuy and the others duly shuffled forward.

As the next band was plugging in and woofing out a couple of quick sound-check chords, the Mare arrived. She ignored two bands that fidgeted on the ramp below the gang, leaping up directly and standing erect beside Qayna.

Chuy shot a nervous glance toward the Bull's throne. The

Bull himself seemed intent on the band now plugging in, as a crowd of women rubbed oil into his left hoof. His eagle-headed companion, though, looked at the bands on the ramp … and maybe at Jane.

"Heads up," Chuy murmured. "We're about to get made."

The eagle-headed Fallen shrieked a wordless cry, and Yamayol turned his head to look at Qayna.

Qayna drew the Calamity Horn.

Eddie pulled the knife from his guitar case and stabbed himself in the arm with it.

What was wrong with Eddie Marlowe?

Chuy clamped his hands over his ears. Seeing him do so, Byl and Joe and Mike followed suit. Twitch screamed, and Jane fired a single shot with the Horn.

She hit Yamayol in the leg. Yamayol bellowed and slipped from his throne, crushing several of his slaves beneath him. Chuy tried to push his way through the bands ahead of him on the ramp, but the wall of human flesh was thick, and Juliana just wasn't strong enough.

Byl was, though. The big guy with the mohawk knotted his fists in front of him and charged the crowd. The other bands, at the same moment, fell apart—some jumped from the ramp, some fell prone, some began screaming, a few took to speaking in tongues.

"Don't worry!" Byl shouted. "I know who the ogre is!"

Joe and Mike and Twitch followed.

Chuy shot a look over his shoulder and saw Qayna swinging into the saddle. The Mare, untroubled by the ravening crowd about her, leaped from the ramp down to the ground, a twenty-foot drop onto asphalt that gave her no trouble at all.

Eddie sank to his knees. He looked up at Chuy and his bad eye suddenly shot sideways.

The blood. The witch in her basement had made Eddie bleed with her chickens, just before he had killed her.

Which must mean she was like Chuy. Or she had become like

Chuy, in that moment. Eddie hadn't killed the witch, he'd brought the witch into his own body. All the grunted dialog since, the eye that didn't move—Missy Broussard had been controlling Eddie's body.

And now, the witch was switching mounts, and moving into …

Chuy turned in time to see the Bull quit bellowing and straighten his back, staring at Eddie.

"That's the witch!" Chuy shouted.

"Yeah." Eddie grunted, struggling to stand. "And me with just this little knife."

The rest of the band fought its way up the ramp. They were attacked by raving musicians, but Byl and Mike were big enough between them to throw the rock and rollers who were actually dangerous off the asphalt.

"This is the witch's plan," Chuy said, thinking out loud. "What does she want?"

"To kill me, I'd say."

The Bull, Yamayol, with the witch Missy Broussard inside, stood. He took two steps to the edge of the spectator box, and then leaped.

"Run!" Chuy grabbed Eddie by the arm and dragged him down the asphalt ramp. The enormous bull-headed man sailed through the air toward them. Chuy knocked aside a keyboardist and a burly man with a Chicago Bears helmet, augmented with three long masonry nails pounded out through its forehead like antlers.

They had reached the first of the school buses when Yamayol hit the bottom of the ramp and ground it to rubble. Chuy dragged Eddie around the bus, ducking and diving into the sheltered spaces surrounded by cheerful yellow metal.

"I get why she wants to kill you," Chuy said. "Why didn't she kill you already? Why not just make you blow your own pinche head off, while you had a shotgun?"

"I resisted," Eddie said. "Turns out I'm a stubborn son of a bitch."

"It would have been helpful if you'd maybe resisted a little earlier," Chuy suggested, "and even said something."

"Lucky me you're so perceptive," Eddie said.

"Yeah, well, I'm a ghost myself," Chuy said. "So no wonder. Plus, the other guys are so excited about the banner. Look at 'em go."

The two peered around the tail end of the bus. They saw their band, close to completing the first circle around the base of the spire.

"Good," Eddie said. "That'll be faster."

"Is it still the plan to get the Ensign, then?"

"That," Eddie said, "and my family."

"Are they here?" Chuy felt embarrassed that he had forgotten.

"In the stand," Eddie said. "I can't be sure I saw my daughters, but I know I saw Sharon."

Yamayol stepped into view, stalking sideways near the bottom of the ramp.

"Pinche mierda!" Chuy pushed Eddie back behind the bus. Chuy heard the thunder of Yamayol's hooves as the Bull rushed in their direction, so he grabbed Eddie and dragged him underneath the bus. Fortunately, Eddie was whipcord thin and didn't resist.

Yamayol staggered to a stop where the two had been standing. He kicked a bus, shattering glass all along one side of it. Then he squatted, grabbed a second bus, and raised its front end off the ground.

Chuy dragged himself out the other side. The crowd roiled, throwing waves of sweaty, mad humanity in several directions. One wave surged up the ramp, throwing musicians off left and right and raging in the direction of the band. A second crept up the front of the spire itself, crawling toward the eagle-headed giantess in the bleachers, shrieking. A third wave rushed toward

Yamayol. Fortunately, it didn't seem to have realized that Eddie and Chuy were Yamayol's prey, so the wave rushed around the two, hiding them. Yamayol turned and trampled his own followers in rage.

Except it wasn't his own followers; the witch was trampling the followers of the Bull.

Eddie pushed his way toward the bandstand and the throne-platform. "Was she already dead, then?"

"Missy Broussard? Maybe. Stories when I was a young man said she'd been around for decades. Could be she was just really old, but it could be she was already a ghost, jumping from one body to another."

"I think if I were her, I might have picked a better-looking body."

Depends, Juliana said. *She looked exactly right for a witch, and that probably got her customers.*

"We need to get that guy's weapons." Eddie pointed at one of the Bull's warriors. The man wore spiked football gear, with a washboard strapped to his chest and back. He had a spear in one hand, a sword at his belt, and a revolver in a holster under one arm. He stood beneath the bandstand, pushing away anxious members of the crowd who tried to climb.

Chuy sniffed. "You're in luck He's bleeding." Juliana's wound, though, had closed. "Give me your knife, cabrón."

Eddie handed over the blade and Chuy cut Juliana's thumb.

Been nice chatting, Juliana told him. *Don't do anything crazy.*

Don't get sentimental. I ain't going anywhere.

Chuy rode the stream of blood out of Juliana's body and into the air. The Bull's warrior was bleeding from his own lip, and Chuy slid inside him. The warrior was focused on defending the struts beneath the stage, jabbing his spear at a ragged trio of men with clubs, and was taken completely by surprise.

"You've seen the menu," Chuy called to Eddie and Juliana. "What do you want?"

"Sword," Eddie said. "I have some experience."

"Better give me the pistol," Juliana said, "because I *don't*."

What is this? the man under Chuy's domination whined.

You are serving the Bull, Chuy told him. *Shut up and pray.*

He passed out the weapons.

CHAPTER EIGHT

C huy examined the tower, looking for a route. The asphalt ramp had lost its lowest fifty feet or so, which meant that it was a twenty-foot vertical jump from the ground to where the ramp now began. That gave some respite to the rest of the band, maybe, in that it cut off the stream of Bull-worshippers who had been pushing up after them—still, a snarling crowd armed with sticks and stones gnawed at their heels, pushing them farther up the ramp.

There was probably a way to climb within the spire; the bottom level looked like it was mostly a museum, cracked and sagging beneath the weight of the tower stacked on its rooftop, despite being reinforced by a series of boxcars welded together and stacked around its sides. And somewhere inside there was supposedly the Sears Tower. But the Bull's followers already swarmed over the boxcars and up through the museum—soon enough they would be a problem for the band, and they were already blocking Chuy's road.

"The stage," Juliana said.

"It's fifteen feet from the stage to the box," Eddie said, "at least."

"But there are cables that connect them," Juliana said.

"Look."

"Could be power cables," Eddie said. "Or audio."

"You have a better plan?" As if to punctuate her question, Juliana fired the pistol. A man wearing a motorcycle helmet with bull's horns painted on it dropped. She picked up his knife and tucked it into her belt.

By way of answer, Eddie started climbing.

Zigzagging iron bars were welded together to make a haphazard maze of struts undergirding the stage, which nestled against the asphalt of the ramp. Eddie went first, then Juliana, and Chuy stood on the ground, poking with his spear anyone who tried to stop them. Eddie pulled himself up to the edge of the stage and was reaching up to get a handhold on the stage itself, with Juliana not far behind, when one of the Bull's fighters dodged a spear attack and wrapped both hands around Chuy's weapon.

"Pinche bastardo." Chuy yanked to free the spear, but in vain, and then someone wrapped his arms around Chuy from behind.

A third man stepped in, swinging something like nunchucks, except that the swinging end had a spiked steel ball.

Time to leave.

No! the Bull's warrior bellowed.

Chuy slipped out through the same split lip by which he had entered.

"No!" the warrior roared out loud now, and the man with the spiky nunchucks hit him in the face.

Chuy turned away as the three attackers stomped their own man to the ground, bellowing and lowing like enraged cattle. None of the three was bleeding, but it was easy enough to find someone who was—only fifty feet away, and desperately trying to climb up support struts to the crumbling foot of the asphalt ramp, was a shirtless man in leather pants, with a machete on his belt and a long scratch up his left arm.

Chuy took the man by surprise and took control easily.

He drew the machete and walked back to the space beneath the stage. Eddie was out of sight now, and Juliana's legs dangled over the edge of the platform as she hauled herself up, too. The Bull's three warriors gripped the lowest struts of the supporting lattice, positioning themselves to climb.

"Ha ha ha," Chuy said. "Well done." He pointed at the dead man on the ground, whose body he had recently inhabited. "There is a madness in the crowd, something that turns men against the Bull."

What are you doing?

"Two escaped," Nunchucks Vato said. "We'll get them."

"Good." Chuy slashed Nunchucks Vato through both hamstrings. He dropped to the gravel, screaming in surprise.

Chuy picked up the nunchucks. When the second of the three men lunged forward as if to take Chuy in a wrestler's grip, Chuy hit him with the nunchucks in the sternum. He fell, chest caved in, and lay still.

The third vato ran.

Chuy tucked the handle of the nunchucks into his belt. It was a wide belt, and a little tight, because the body he was in was a little portly. The leather pants were sticky with sweat and scratched his borrowed flesh as he moved, and the sharp points of the nunchucks dug into his skin, but Chuy began climbing up the struts.

What monster are you? the possessed man asked.

I'm no monster, Chuy said. *You've just gone crazy.*

Chuy felt tears running down his borrowed cheeks.

He was just below the level of the stage when Juliana scooted into view. She lay on her belly and leaned over the stage, head and arms visible, and she pointed her pistol at Chuy. "Tell me your name, big guy, or I drop you."

"Pinche cretina, you know my name. This is Chuy, and I was driving your chassis twenty minutes ago. I gave you that pistol, because you didn't know how to use a sword."

"You had me at pinche cretina," she said. "You need a hand?"

"I don't," Chuy grunted, "but this fat bastard does."

Hey!

Juliana extended a hand.

"Are you braced?" Chuy asked.

"If you fall and die, do you care?"

"No," Chuy admitted, "but it would be a shame if you fell, too."

"Aw, Chuy, you care about me. I'm braced."

He took Juliana's hand, and she helped him navigate over a tricky stretch with bad handholds. Then he was at the lip of the stage, and she and Eddie were both there, pulling him up to safety. The stage was a mess; amplifiers knocked over and buzzing, one decapitated corpse lying across a soundboard and two severed arms on the floor.

"Look." Chuy pointed. "Just in time."

The rest of the band, other than Qayna, had completed a loop around the spire and was approaching the stage. A gangplank had been fashioned to connect the ramp to the stage by laying an aluminum ladder flat across the gap between them and strapping it into place on the stage side. The band advanced with Byl and Joe at the front; Byl had a two-by-four and was swinging it like he had the tetsubo, side to side relentlessly, sweeping the path in front of them, and occasionally bringing the plank around for an overhand blow when one of the Bull-worshippers resisted. Joe had found a pair of revolvers and had one in each hand. He advanced steadily, shouting "Yee ha!" each time he fired. His left-hand shots seemed to go wide of their targets, but as he was firing into a mob, he hit bad guys anyway.

"Maybe someone should teach Joe a little fire discipline," Chuy suggested.

"Never interrupt your ally when he's kicking ass," Eddie said. "No matter how he's doing it."

Chuy led the charge across the ladder-walkway, swinging the spiked chainstick. He conked two Bull-worshippers before they even saw him, and the gap he created made a third vato fall.

Juliana fired repeatedly into the side of the mob, and by the time that Eddie got across the ladder with his sword, the front ranks had crumpled into the resulting gap, pushed by Joe and Byl, and were turning to run.

Joe and Juliana then charged the mob on the other side, bringing relief to Mike and Twitch. The sudden onslaught, with sounds of gunshots, made that crowd fall back, too, and the band had a moment of peace.

"We're going for the Ensign," Byl said.

Eddie nodded.

"I think we should consider crossing one of these struts and getting into the tower itself," Joe said. "The building blocks here are smaller than they were below, houses and cars. I'm pretty sure we can climb up faster than we can march, especially with those guys fighting us."

"Don't consider it," Eddie said. "Do it."

"Where did the big eagle-headed one go?" Mike asked.

Chuy looked at the throne-platform and saw that his brother was right; warriors of the Bull crowded a group of prisoners into one corner of the stand, but the two Fallen were gone. He looked down to the ground and found them.

"She's with Yamayol. They're going through the crowd, killing people. Eddie, get down. The last thing we need is for them to come charging up here."

Eddie crouched, dropping out of sight. "I'm going after Sharon."

"We can get the Ensign, no problem." Joe grinned as he stuffed more shells into his pistols.

"I am a little disappointed that the concert never happened," Byl said. "This would have been my biggest gig ever."

"Unpaid gig," Juliana said, "in front of a crowd of insane cultists, with a chance that the club owner kills you on the spot."

"No gig is perfect," Byl said.

"I'm with Eddie," Chuy said.

"Me too." Juliana nodded. "You guys are having the most

fun. Also, rescuing people is right up my alley."

She looked at Chuy as she said it and he felt himself blushing.

Who are you guys?

We're like the pinche Red Cross, Chuy said. *But with guns and electric guitars.*

Before the mob to either side could return, Joe led the way across a thick steel girder and into the body of the spire. Mike and Twitch followed him, and Byl came last. The big man lingered on the girder awhile with his two-by-four, batting several attackers off and to the ground. When he finally retreated into the tower, climbing up through the seats of a passenger train car as if they were the rungs of a ladder, Joe rained bullets down on the girder to cover his retreat.

In the meantime, Juliana had untied the ladder-bridge and withdrawn it onto the stage.

"You know knots," Eddie said.

"We were a scouting family," she said. "Before it all hit the fan."

Chuy scanned the throne-platform. The prisoners huddled in the corner were mostly women and children, and they were unarmed. They had dog collars on their necks, but they weren't chained; men with spears and spiked armor kept them in their place. Other men, with maces and swords and clubs and spears, stood at the edge of the platform, uneasily watching Eddie and his companions.

And one of them had a thick bundle of rope coiled over his shoulder. Maybe his job was to rope the prisoners—the slaves?—in a line and bring them to and from the platform, but the whys and wherefores certainly didn't matter to Chuy.

He picked a target and nudged Juliana. "Can you shoot that guy?" He pointed. "In the leg or the arm, if you can. Don't kill him."

Juliana nodded. "One steed for Chuy, coming right up. And what about your current horse?"

"Do what you have to do." Chuy tossed the nunchucks to the ground beside Eddie, who picked them up.

Juliana drew a bead on the man Chuy had indicated, a burly guy with a kukri. *Bam!*

She hit him in the thigh, and he staggered back, cursing and clapping a hand to the wound.

Chuy exited the scratch in his man's arm.

Juliana turned and pressed the muzzle of her pistol to the man's forehead. "You can jump, or I can shoot. If you jump, you might survive."

"I might not!" the man gasped.

"Bend your knees when you hit," she advised him.

He cursed, but began lowering himself over the edge of the stage to drop to the ground.

Chuy crossed the gap from the stage to the throne-platform. The wounded Kukri Vato lay on his back right next to the guy with the coil of rope; Rope Vato knelt and wrapped a pocket bandanna around the wound.

Chuy entered Kukri Vato and took control.

What's that? Kukri Vato asked.

Chuy ignored him. With the kukri, he reached over and casually scratched Rope Vato's leg.

"You son of a bitch!" Rope Vato slapped Kukri Vato, but Chuy had already exited, and was slipping into Rope Vato through the scratch.

He took control and grabbed the kukri. Kukri Vato, disoriented from the brief experience of possession, lay stunned and gasping, and Chuy sank the kukri into his neck.

Then he stood up and stepped back. Bull-worshippers glared at him under their helmets, and he glared back. "He attacked me!"

They muttered and spat and went back to staring at Eddie.

Chuy had no experience with ropes. He couldn't tie a knot to save his life, and he certainly couldn't tie a lasso.

Here's the deal, ese, Chuy said. *You seem like a practical guy.*

You're going to tie the end of the rope to the corner of the platform over there, and then you're going to throw the rope to my friends on the stage.

That seems like a stupid move for me to make, Rope Vato said. *I'm not gonna do it.*

I understand, Chuy said. *But see how we're holding a kukri in our hands?* He held it up close to Rope Vato's face so the man could see the blade. *I'll give you a little control of your arms, and if you don't tie the rope and throw it like I told you, then I will cut off your balls.*

You'll just kill me anyway, once your friends are over here.

Chuy liked Rope Vato, he had guts. *I understand your concern. You see that vato over there, who just dropped to the ground?*

I think he broke his leg, Rope Vato pointed out.

Yeah, sucks for him. But he's alive. We want to spare people. I want to spare people. That was the guy whose body I was in two minutes ago. It could be you, two minutes from now.

Rope Vato hesitated for a moment.

Okay, I'll do it.

Chuy walked over to the corner of the throne-platform. Here, a length of steel pole that held up this corner of the former bleachers, jutting out from the body of the tower, rose above the steel floor and bent back inward, creating a hook or an anchor. Chuy relaxed his control.

This is it, he warned Rope Vato. *No false moves.*

Rope Vato threw the rope over the platform and watched it fall to the ground.

Chuy slammed his control back on the traitor. *You lying son of a bitch.*

I can live without my balls.

"Is everything okay over there, Carl?" one of the Bull-worshippers called. The vato wore overalls and held a baseball bat with nails through it.

Chuy gave the man a thumbs up. "Accident!" he called. "I meant to tie it as a way for us to get down."

"We don't leave the throne until the Bull moves us." Overalls Vato crossed his arms over his chest and looked proud.

What an idiot.

He's doing his duty, Rope Vato said. *He serves the Bull.*

Doing your duty to a country I get, Chuy said. *That makes you a patriot. Doing your duty to a giant asshole with a bull's head who is literally one of the chief demons of Hell just makes you a moron.*

Eddie and Juliana stood on the stage, staring helplessly.

Chuy looked at the tower. There was no staircase or ladder per se, but the tower itself was climbable. You didn't even need to cross a strut to get to it; the back of the throne-platform was bolted to the side of a tractor trailer, you could just climb over the top of the truck and into what looked like the crumpled remains of a diner.

He saw Byl and Joe and the others climbing. Their pursuit was far behind but gaining quickly, and the band was getting closer to the standard-bearer. The caterpillar rider bounced in an agitated fashion, the banner trembling.

What was Eddie Marlowe going to do with the banner? Something that Heaven wanted him to do, apparently.

Something like what the Bull had done, only maybe a nicer version?

Chuy wasn't entirely sure about the Ensign. But he did want to save Eddie's family.

He walked up to Overalls Vato. "Hey, ese," he said. "Can I see your club? I want to see what kind of baseball bat you have going on there."

"Ese?" Overalls Vato frowned.

Shit. Chuy hit the vato once in the neck with his kukri and took the bat from the man's numb hands as he slumped to the floor.

The other Bull-worshippers weren't watching him, and didn't immediately notice what he had done; some were jeering at Eddie, and four of them held spears on the knot of prisoners in the corner.

Chuy walked up behind the Spear Vatos. At the last second, one of them turned around, and Chuy hit him in the shoulder with the spiked bat. The other three turned, and Chuy slashed one across the face with his kukri, pushing the man back and making him knock over one of his friends, like two falling dominos.

The fourth man leaped forward, but two of the prisoners, a burly woman and a thin man with wild eyes, grabbed him. As the rest of the Bull-worshippers on the platform finally realized what was happening and feet pounded on the steel floor, the two prisoners stripped the spear from the man's hands and hurled him from the platform.

There were a dozen prisoners on the stand; six of them were children.

The adults snatched up spears, and Chuy handed one the spiked club, keeping the kukri for himself. The prisoners stepped forward, putting up a ragged fence of spearpoints, but it was enough to make the Bull-worshippers stop their charge.

Bam! As the Bull-worshippers hesitated, Juliana fired into them. There was no cover on the platform, and after she had dropped two, the others fled, jumping to the ground to escape.

"I'm here with Eddie Marlowe." Chuy pointed across the gap at the stage. "We've come to rescue all of you, but especially his family. Sharon, right? And two girls?"

A strong-jawed black woman—one of the prisoners who had picked up a spear—raised a cautious hand. "I'm Sharon."

Two young women crowded close to her. All three wore simple shifts and smelled of oil and cattle musk.

Chuy looked over to Eddie for guidance. Eddie was looking suddenly in a different direction; following his gaze, Chuy saw the two Fallen. They had spotted Eddie and Juliana and were charging toward them.

Eddie waved Chuy away, and pointed up the tower.

"Okay," Chuy said. "Eddie's going to join us in a minute. Who's up for a little climb?"

CHAPTER NINE

Y ou're being quiet because you want me to forget that I promised
to castrate you, Chuy said. You think I'll just let you go. Well, I
won't.

Rope Vato said nothing.

They climbed up a large playground jungle gym. The metal
poles and bars were Christmas green, the plastic slides and
cabins and bridge planks were dump-truck yellow, and the
webbing and climbing-wall handholds were brick red.

"Tell me your names," Chuy said to Eddie's girls, trying to
distract them from the fact that they were climbing up a plastic
rope bridge over a hundred-foot fall.

Sharon interposed herself, climbing ahead of her daughters,
all three gripped to the plastic rope. "So you are who, exactly?
One of Yamayol's men, but a friend of my ex-husband?"

Chuy took a deep breath. "This is really none of my business,
but if you say ex-husband, that's going to make him feel really
bad."

"Correct, it is none of your business."

"Okay, I don't really know the details, because I joined the
band late, but Eddie—"

"Band? My husband left us for a band? He wasn't even a good guitar player."

Chuy laughed. "Yeah, that was the problem. Okay, no frills story time. He went to a witch here in Chicago who was going to help him get good on the guitar. She sent him down to the cross-roads, like they say, and he met a demon there. Only part of what happened is he started seeing visions of you and the girls dying, and in his visions, he was always present, so he left."

"He left to protect us?" one of the girls asked.

"Dumbass," Sharon muttered.

"Yeah," Chuy said, "and yeah. And when he stopped having those visions, he came back, to be with you, and, as it happens, to rescue you. On the way, he killed the witch, and her ghost is now possessing Yamayol. And if you look down there, you can see Yamayol, only it's really the witch, trying to stomp Eddie dead in payback."

Sharon looked. Wind whipped around the spire and both their faces, but Chuy thought he saw a glisten in her eyes that at least hinted at tears.

"Wow," one of the girls said. "Dad's pretty fast."

"Look, it's not really in my nature to compliment people," Chuy said. "But he's a pretty good dude."

Sharon shook her head. "So you were in his rock and roll band. He was the shitty guitar player, so you were the shitty drummer or something. And then you went undercover in Yamayol's kingdom to rescue us."

Chuy laughed. "It's so much more complicated than that. No, I'm the dead brother of the shitty bass player. And when Eddie and the band went down to Hell and came back out again, they brought me with them. And this body isn't my body, this body belongs to some vato who happened to be on the platform with you when I needed to get there. So before we're done, you're likely going to see me jump into someone else's body. Only to you it will probably just look like some new person says, 'Hey, I'm Chuy.' Also, you'll see me castrate this guy."

"Ew," one of the girls said.

"You're not a *nice* man, then," Sharon observed.

"Well, I promised him I would do it," Chuy said. "I was sentenced to Hell, but that doesn't mean I don't try to keep my word."

So admirable. You bastard.

"I'm Bessie," the older girl said.

"I'm Billie," said the younger.

"Oh, good," Chuy said. "Both B-names. That will make it easy to remember."

"They're named after classic blues singers," Sharon said.

"I didn't think humans were named Bessie," Chuy said. "I thought that was a name only cows had. Like Rex and dogs. And the only Billy I can think of off the top of my head is Billy Dee Williams."

"A *Star Wars* actor. And you have a *Star Wars* name."

"Ha ha, no, Chuy, C-H-U-Y, not C-H-E-W-I-E, like the Wookiee. Chuy is a nickname. It's short for Jesus."

"So you're Latino."

"Yeah, Chicano, whatever. My family is from Mexico. Archuleta, that's our name. Juarez, El Paso, Las Cruces, that area. My brother Mike, the bassist, is really Miguel. He's not real comfortable with being Mexican, just like he's not real comfortable with being gay."

They scampered up a slab of concrete, clinging to the rebar shafts that protruded from it. What had this been, before it was uprooted and shoved into the tower?

"Is your brother one of those people?" Sharon pointed, and Chuy saw the band. They were all still there, looking battered but grimly determined. They were backing up the tower parallel to Chuy and the freed prisoners, slowed by the fact that spike-bristling, club- and axe-armed warriors of the Bull yapped at their heels. Byl and Mike defended the rear; Byl still swung his timber with two hands, his hips and legs wedged into the tight space between two cars to hold him in place, and Mike had a length of two-inch pipe in each hand.

"Yeah," Chuy said. "See the two big vatos? The smaller one, the guy without the mohawk, that's Mike."

"And bigger guy?"

"We picked him up locally. He's a tailor or something."

"They're trapped."

Chuy looked closer; it was true. Twitch and Joe were scrambling, trying to find a way up the tower, but the path forward was blocked by the roof shingles of a small rambler, squatting upside down between two chunks of asphalt. They'd climbed into a dead end. And Joe wasn't shooting anymore. He'd liked it so much, that must mean he'd run out of bullets.

Mike and Byl looked tired.

Chuy sighed. "Okay, I'm going to go help those guys. This body—you're safest if you just kill it right away. I'll have to break my promise to geld him, but I can get another body over there, for sure."

"Look!" Bessie pointed. A length of corrugated pipe had one open mouth near them, and it sagged along the side of a cracked bridge but then rose, opening its other mouth just to the side of the Bull-worshippers who were throwing themselves against Mike and Byl. The pipe was five and a half feet tall, tall enough to walk through.

"We can all go," Billie said.

"Some of you are kids," Chuy said hesitantly.

"He's right," Sharon said. "Kids to the rear." Bessie and Billie looked defiant but did as she said, falling back.

Sharon took the lead. The three other freed prisoners with spears went with her first, points forward, into the pipe.

"Pinche cretinos." Chuy followed, and at his side came the freed prisoner holding the spiked baseball bat.

Chuy worried that the pipe wouldn't hold them, but it didn't so much as sag or groan as the six armed people crept quickly down through it and then up again. The children came behind them, with the seventh adult, a white-haired Asian man who had, since the rescue, armed himself with a splintering timber. As they neared the far end, the sounds of fighting got louder, and Chuy could hear Mike.

"Huevos!" his brother shouted. Dumbass, weak-sounding cussing, but it was one of his brother's favorites, along with *mierda* and *hodido.*

But Mike had rescued Chuy, and it was only fair that, dipshit that his brother was, Chuy should now rescue Mike.

"On three," Sharon whispered. "One, two, three!"

They charged. The former prisoners with the spears slammed into the Bull-worshippers from the side. Two men in leather jackets with axes were impaled, one through the chest and the other through the leg, causing both of them to fall and bounce down the tower and out of sight. One of them pulled the spear with him as he fell. A third was scratched deeply across both buttocks, and turned to flee. A fourth took the spiked baseball bat to the side of his head and fell still. Chuy threw himself upon the others, hacking at arms and chests and screaming until the Bull's men fell back, scrambling across a jumble of cinderblocks and a thicket of shopping carts to get away.

Byl was panting, and raised his two-by-four over his head. "I hope one of you is Chuy."

"I am," Chuy said.

"I'm Sharon," Sharon added. "I think you know my husband, Eddie."

"We like Eddie," Joe said. "He let us join his band."

"Yeah, but he's going to make you be the keyboardist," Byl said.

"Using the keyboard as a tool does not make me a keyboard player." Joe smiled, showing lots of teeth. "You guys don't look like you're carrying spare bullets in your pockets."

"Is there a way up through that pipe?" Twitch bounded down from the shingled barrier. Chuy nodded, but Twitch hadn't waited for an answer; she was already scooting past the children and into the tall pipe.

Chuy stopped at the mouth of the pipe to see what was happening with Eddie. The guitar player was dodging among the struts beneath the stage, which had been smashed to ruins. He had a sword in his hand, and seemed surprisingly comfortable with it, slashing from time to time at the ankles of the Bull or the Eagle. Juliana, too, sheltered among the stage supports and fired her pistol. She fired at the Fallen, but she also shot at the crowd. Surrounding the disintegrating stage, a rabble with sticks and stones and knives and spears surged forward from time to time to attack the two guitar players. They were kept from bum-rushing the scene by the fact that, when any of them got too close, they got trodden upon by the Fallen, and if they escaped being flattened by hoof or torn apart by talon, Juliana shot them.

But the two Fallen were shredding the stage, piece by piece, and would surely, at any moment, get Eddie. Only a quarter of the platform remained, and Yamayol strained to rip a piece off at that moment, trying to get at the humans beneath.

"You guys get the Ensign," Chuy said to Byl and Mike, who were bringing up the rear.

"Where you going?" Mike asked.

Chuy sighed. "Looks like someone has to save Eddie. Again."

He slashed his borrowed body across the thigh and blood welled out. *No time to keep my promise, chingón. Enjoy the ride.*

He handed the kukri to Mike, and jumped off the tower.

As Chuy exited the body through the blood flowing out its thigh, Rope Vato screamed. Chuy dove, willing himself to fall faster and regretting the almost leisurely drift as he moved across the open space between himself and the scene of combat below.

He smelled blood coming from all the participants. For a moment, he fell toward Juliana, imagining helping her make better shot selection, and maybe shooting the Fallen in the eyes.

Only she was doing just fine, and was only inflicting limited wounds on the Fallen because they were both so big and tough.

He should enter one of the Fallen. And the witch Missy Broussard was inside Yamayol. So he should take the eagle-headed woman.

Except then he'd have to attack Yamayol. Whereas if he would take over the Bull, he might be able to save Eddie by simply running away.

Rope Vato hit the side of a Greyhound bus embedded into the base of the tower. He burst like a water balloon.

Chuy dove through a bullet wound in Yamayol's side into the Bull's body.

What he found was a tangled mess. He didn't have words to describe what it was like inside other humans, or animals, or even monsters like the flying bats, but there was order. There were moving parts, and they went together, and there were natural connectors. When part of the body moved, the other parts all reacted, and in synch with the soul that was inside. It was easy for Chuy to ride along with that soul, even when the form wasn't human.

The inside of the Bull seemed kluged together. It was like looking under the hood of an old car and finding that the engine had been rebuilt, but entirely out of parts tooled from soup cans and strapped together with duct tape. It all clanked and ground together with a screeching sound when it moved. Physical parts that were never meant to be joined were welded together with sutures of blood and pain, but spiritual parts, too, were stapled to the monstrous, staggering whole.

Chuy felt sick. The Bull was an abomination, a crime against the world.

But there at the center of all the clicking, howling, grinding parts, was a bright point of light. From the light emanated blue strings, each string shooting out individually to a single piece of Yamayol. A shadow hovered above that light, tugging at strings and gazing into the point to judge reaction.

A shadow in the shape of Missy Broussard.

She didn't see Chuy coming. He slammed into her side, sending her skittering between a shoulder and an ancient grudge, both connected to the point of light and webbed to each other with a swampy black shadow. Chuy looked into the light and found strings that looked like legs and vocal cords.

He staggered away from the stage, dropping his hands to his side and releasing the metal his body had been trying to rip. The eagle-headed woman stared at him.

"Eddie!" he roared. "This is Chuy! Sharon and the girls are safe! Bilbo and Betty both!"

Eddie stared up, astonished, but only for a moment. "Get the Ensign!" he yelled. "Command the crowd. Nothing wins here but the Ensign to the Nation!"

"Stop!" the eagle-headed woman cried.

Chuy ran. In two steps, he crossed the ground to the bottom of the ramp. Leaping over the rubble, he was easily able to drag himself onto the bottom lip of the spiraling asphalt. As he pulled his legs up and onto the ramp, two things hit him at the same moment.

In the body of Yamayol that he possessed, the eagle-headed Fallen leaped upon him. She grabbed his hips and dragged, trying to pull him down off the ramp. "Who are you?" the Eagle shrieked, eyes glittering.

Within the body, the witch hit Chuy from the side, knocking him away from the point of light. He bounced off the hard, nutty shells of a cluster that felt like regrets, buried deep within Yamayol, and came to rest against an enormous, rapidly thudding heart.

The witch ignored Yamayol for a moment, and the Bull himself took over again. "Get back, woman!" he bellowed, and he kicked the Eagle in the shoulder. The Eagle crashed down into a sitting position, perplexity and hurt on her face.

The witch leaped at Chuy, teeth glittering long and white in the shadow within the Bull.

Yamayol climbed to his feet on the ramp.

Chuy leaped aside. He grabbed the shade of Missy Broussard by her long hair and slammed his knee into her chin. She fell among the Bull's grinding flesh gears, stunned, and Chuy reached again into the point of light to seize the reins.

"I'm Jesus Archuleta, bitch!" he shouted. "Your time has come!"

He took two running steps up the winding ramp and leaped onto the tower.

He had yelled at the Fallen because he wanted her to follow him, rather than turn and attack Eddie and Juliana. Follow him she did, springing up the spire and hissing, an angry sound like water on a hot frying pan.

The spire had seemed enormous to Chuy when he was in the body of other humans. Now that he was in the body of the Bull, it seemed merely large. Gaps in the construction that were impassible barriers to Mike and Twitch were footholds to the body of Yamayol, and he hurled himself up the tower as quickly as he could.

He was careful not to put his enormous, borrowed hands and especially his hooves anywhere where there was a climbing human. The Eagle was not nearly so polite, and her talons tore and impaled men on the tower; her recklessness gave her speed, and she gained quickly.

But then Chuy arrived. The band, and the free prisoners with them, fought against the standard-bearer on his caterpillar. The standard-bearer was on a flat space like a parking lot, connecting the ramp and the spire, which allowed him to put his back against a literal red-brick wall. Backed against the wall, he still seemed to be winning—Mike lay bleeding, two of the freed prisoners lay dead, and the caterpillar held Twitch in two of its legs, wrapping her in something like a web.

"Out of the way!" Chuy yelled—

and the witch hit him again.

He fell, icy pain spearing his side. He was leaking ... blood?

93

Spirit? The witch had punctured his integrity. He hadn't realized that was even possible.

"Holy shit," Chuy muttered, touching a hand to his ghostly side. The effluent was ice-cold.

He shook his head. The witch had taken control. Yamayol bent and snatched up Byl in one hand and Joe in the other. His mouth gaped and he breathed out steam and he roared into both their faces, "You die for helping Eddie Marlowe!"

Eagle head grabbed the Bull's shoulder. "You die for this, sorcerer Jesus!" she shrieked, and plunged her beak into Yamayol's shoulder.

The witch didn't drop Byl and Joe, but she turned, stumbling. She was distracted, but Chuy felt weak. He didn't think he could knock her from the control position again.

But as the Bull staggered around, he saw two things. He saw that Yamayol now danced beside the standard-bearer. The armored man on the caterpillar no doubt thought Yamayol was simply his master, and was unaware of the battle raging within the Fallen, because he moved from side to side to avoid being trampled and continued to fight the spear- and club-wielding humans before him.

And Chuy also saw how Yamayol's legs worked. Lines of control, lines of ancient words chanted and also written in blood, ran down through a knot of ambition and a pelvis that looked part human, and part dinosaur fossil, into the immense, pumping thews of the bull-headed giant.

Chuy threw himself into the knot of ambition, gripped one of the cords, and pulled.

The Bull's leg jerked up spasmodically—

and kicked the standard-bearer off his mount.

Yamayol fell, crashing onto his back on the carpet of asphalt.

The Ensign to the Nations missed the asphalt and went tumbling down the tower.

CHAPTER TEN

The Ensign's pole struck the concrete curve of a geodesic
dome protruding from the side of the tower and bounced.
It rose, shivered, and then tipped forward in a somersaulting
motion. The leaves of the green bough at the tip of the Ensign
fluttered, and then the standard went spinning toward the
ground end over end.

Chuy wanted to watch the Ensign, wanted to do something
to make sure it bounced in the direction of Eddie and Juliana,
but he couldn't, because the Eagle was pouncing on him.

For a split second, he nearly abandoned Yamayol and simply
fled. But he was too close to Byl, Joe, Mike, and Twitch, and if
Yamayol and the eagle-headed giantess thrashed about on the
asphalt ramp—no matter who was making the decisions for the
Bull—they might crush his friends.

The witch was howling curses at Chuy, but he was still in
control of the legs. He tugged the knees in tight, pressing them
hard and fast against the Bull's chest, and then he kicked straight
out.

The hooves struck the Eagle, one in the center of her forehead
and the other against a shoulder. Her forward momentum
reversed abruptly and she flew back against the spire, landing in

a crouch with her shoulders against a knot of muscle cars. Yamayol slid along the asphalt, pushed like a sledge by the Eagle's blow, and Chuy felt the Bull teeter at the edge of the ramp.

He also felt Byl and Twitch hitting Yamayol's flank.

Someone was shoving a steel pole beneath Yamayol's shoulder. That was Joe, and he had a barrel, no, a big metal spool, and Mike threw it beneath the pole.

You worthless shit! Missy Broussard shrieked. She sprang upon him, slashing with nails like daggers.

Joe yelled for help. Byl and Twitch and Mike threw themselves onto the end of his lever and pulled. The Bull's body began to lift.

Chuy dragged one more time on Yamayol's soul-tendons, making the Bull kick against the tower itself, and Yamayol slid backward again.

And then fell.

He dropped headfirst toward the ground. He saw the massed crowd, the shattered and enraged mob that had once been Chicago, rising and rushing toward the tower. He saw Eddie and Juliana, struggling against a knot of Bull-worshippers for the Ensign; Juliana shot two men, Eddie ran one through, and then they both grabbed the pole at the same moment as another pair of men in spiked Bears helmets. Chuy felt the witch slice into his ghostly flesh again and he screamed, but then he pushed himself out one of the Bull's wounds, and was free and alone on the side of the spire.

Yamayol crashed into the crowd atop a dozen people, flattening them. Then he stood, his motions stiff. Was the witch still in control?

Eddie throat punched one of the two men facing him and Juliana shot the other in the chest. They stepped back and raised the Ensign to the Nations as they would a spear, pointing its tip toward the Bull.

The Eagle dropped from the tower, falling the height—one

hundred fifty feet, or two hundred?—and landing smoothly on her feet.

The mob closed in on all sides, shouting.

"I am Yamayol," the Bull bellowed. Chuy could barely hear the Fallen over the yelling of the crowd. "I am the god of this city. All bow down."

"You are not!" the Eagle cried. "You are an enemy, lodged in the breast of the Bull. I can free the Bull, but only after we have dragged Yamayol's body to the ground. Subdue your lord, my people! He is ill, and I can save him!"

Chuy felt weak and sick. He settled onto a spiral staircase that wound down through one side of the tower. He couldn't take deep breaths to calm the feelings of nausea and debilitation, but he flattened himself against the steps and tried to relax.

He heard Eddie Marlowe shout. "And he will lift up an ensign to the nations from far, and will hiss unto them from the end of the earth: and, behold, they shall come with speed swiftly! None shall be weary nor stumble among them; none shall slumber nor sleep; neither shall the girdle of their loins be loosed, nor the latchet of their shoes be broken!"

The crowd fell silent.

"Thief!" the Eagle cried.

"Yamayol was a thief!" Eddie shouted. "He claimed authority that was not his, because he wanted power. All his power was stolen, all his words lies! But the Word has been borne to me, and Heaven has commanded that I take up this banner. Whose arrows are sharp, and all their bows bent, their horses' hooves shall be counted like flint, and their wheels like a whirlwind!"

Footsteps on the staircase made Chuy look up; Sharon and her daughters led the way down, and behind them came the other freed prisoners and the band.

Chuy felt light, and getting lighter. He felt that a strong breeze might blow him away entirely, but he smelled blood. Reaching out and finding the flow, he rode it to its source, and found himself inside one of Eddie's daughters.

Don't be afraid, he said. *I'm Chuy.*

What's a Chuy? she asked. *Do you mean that ghost Mom was talking to?*

Yes. Are you … Bunny? he guessed. *Becky?*

Billie. I don't want to be possessed.

I'm not going to possess you. I just need … a ride.

Well, don't go dying, either. The last thing I want is dead ghost clutter stuck inside me forever.

"Mom," she said, "I've got Chuy."

Sharon stopped to give Chuy a piercing glance. "Are you controlling my daughter?"

"No, Mom, this is Billie talking. He's just … here. I think he's hurt."

I am hurt.

"Well, don't take any crap from him," Sharon said. "Just because he's hurt, doesn't mean he gets to take liberties."

Below, the mob hesitated.

Yamayol lunged at Eddie, but the Eagle was faster. She grabbed his calves from behind and dragged him to the ground. Pouncing upon him, she thumped him between the shoulders, and then sang a high-pitched, keening melody without words.

Eddie kept shouting. "Their roaring shall be like a lion, they shall roar like young lions: yea, they shall roar, and lay hold of the prey, and shall carry it away safe, and none shall deliver it."

The Ensign to the Nations was rustling. Billie kept her eyes on where she was putting her feet, which was wise, but Chuy could still look out her peripheral vision and see that the crowd stared at Eddie, transfixed, and the banner moved.

The bough at its tip blew out sideways, as if in a gentle breeze, and although the sky was overcast and gray, the bough seemed to be bathed in sunlight.

Yamayol rolled sideways, partially dislodging the Eagle and crushing several men standing at the fringes of the crowd. When the Eagle struck again with her fists, he grabbed a forearm, dragged it to his mouth, and bit her.

Oh no, she's changing bodies!

Who's changing bodies? Billie asked.

There's a witch inside the bull-headed giant. Yamayol. And she's a ghost, like me, and I think she's about to jump —

Into the bird-head.

I need to borrow your mouth, just to yell a warning.

Do it.

"Eddie!" Chuy yelled, using Billie's lungs to their full force and capacity. "The witch is jumping bodies!"

Eddie ignored him. "And in that day," he yelled, raising the banner as high as he could, "they shall roar against them like the roaring of the sea: and if one look unto the land, behold darkness and sorrow, and the light is darkened in the heavens thereof."

The mob roared.

The Eagle stood up and stepped away. Yamayol lay on his back, looking stunned and defeated.

"Detain them both!" Eddie shouted.

The mob rushed forward. They threw ropes over Yamayol, subduing him, and they flung themselves on the legs of the Eagle, trying to drag her down. She slashed with talons and swung fists like wrecking balls, but there were thousands of people, and they would drag her down.

Only it wouldn't matter. Because once they captured that body, the witch would simply exit it and enter any one of the thousand human bodies in the press, and then quietly walk away.

Did he care? He found that he did.

He exited through a cut in Billie's knee. Once he was no longer being carried, he felt weak again. Desiccated, shriveled, emptying. He felt like a balloon that had slowly lost all its air and now lay on the floor, a deflated white avocado.

Could he die? What would he leave behind if he did?

Chuy raced downward.

He had no way to see the witch's shade, once she exited the

Fallen's body, but if he could intercept her before she left, she'd be visible....

And then what?

He had no idea how she had wounded him. He had no idea how he could possibly wound her.

And he felt weaker by the second.

"Qayna!" Eddie shouted. "The one they call Crow Jane! Brother-slayer, avenger of innocence, first witness and first criminal! Come, I bid you!"

Eddie's voice sounded preternaturally loud. Was this the effect of Chuy's imminent destruction, that his mind was distorting his perceptions? Or did the Ensign to the Nations magnify Eddie's voice?

Chuy dropped into the body of the Eagle through her wounded forearm. The Fallen grabbed two warriors from the crowd, one in each hand; the man in her left was wrapped in practice pads from a wrestling club or karate dojo and held an axe handle, and the man in her right had a sharpened boathook. Both men swung their weapons at her.

Crouched over the pinprick dot of light that was the Fallen's soul, the witch scarcely had to manipulate the Fallen to get the result she wanted. A subtle touch to two strings of light, and the Fallen cracked the two men together, vaporizing both their heads in clouds of blood.

The witch turned to face Chuy. Her nails and teeth were long and yellow and dripped dark ichor. She neglected to control the Fallen, but it waded into the mob, continuing to grab and slash and bite.

You're one of the damned. Her voice had curl and smoke in it.

I was. Chuy moved in closer to her, standing on a bladder of bile and preparing to leap if she moved.

Then you still are, in this world, the witch said. *You always will be. You don't belong here among the living.*

Do you?

Only until I kill Eddie Marlowe. I saw him coming for me on the very day I brought him to the crossroads to meet the Bull.

If you saw Eddie coming for you eventually, then why do it? Why take him down to the crossroads? Why not just tell him to piss off, go learn to play guitar the hard way?

He was determined, Broussard said *And the alternatives were worse.*

Are you saying you had no choice? Chuy asked.

I'm saying I did have a choice, the witch said. *And I chose with more insight and foresight than most of us are ever allowed to do, and I made the best choice I could at the time, and here we are.*

Ropes were being thrown over the Eagle, but the witch seemed to ignore them. Chuy thought he heard the snorting of the Mare.

And now? Chuy asked. *Are you making your best choice now? Is there some redemption for you, if you kill Eddie Marlowe?*

There is no redemption, the witch hissed. *Not for me, not for you, not for anyone. But there is victory. Eddie Marlowe is a two-bit, no-account grifter who lucked into a marriage over his station and over his head, and it will not be said in Chicago that he defeated Missy Broussard.*

The Eagle shook as the mob pulled her to her knees. Limbs and energy lines and old hatreds and forgotten deeds trembled and slammed against each other, and the witch looked back down at the dot at the center of the Fallen.

And Chuy leaped.

He had no attack that could harm her, but he wrapped his arms around her, locked his hands behind her back, and squeezed.

What are you doing? the witch shrieked.

My brother tried to save me, Chuy shouted back. *Maybe he failed. Maybe it was a stupid, impossible idea from the start. Now is my chance to try to pay him back.*

The witch bent her legs, raising her knees sideways. This drew her body closer into Chuy's, and he felt revulsion mixed with his ebbing vitality. Then she dug toenails into his hips and dragged her feet down along him.

Chuy screamed, and his scream was so loud, the Fallen screamed with him.

The crowd, following Eddie's shouted directions, dragged the Eagle to the ground and bound her.

Chuy's arms were weak and he felt as if he were melting. *How do you feel about press-ups, bitch?* he snarled into Missy Broussard's face.

She sneered, and he threw them both down. They struck the elephantine heart of the Fallen, bounced once—

and then froze.

Chuy tried to move his arms and couldn't. The witch hissed.

"Come out!" a voice commanded.

Chuy and Missy Broussard trickled from the arm wound of the gigantic Fallen. Chuy now saw that the Eagle lay on a circle, chalked into the gravel; the fact that the crowd stared at him and the witch made him realize that he was visible to them, floating above the body of the giant eagle-headed woman.

The voice doing the commanding was that of Qayna. She stood beside Eddie with her arms raised, duster sleeves falling open to reveal tattooed characters on her arms to match those on her face. Juliana stood behind them, holding the reins to the Mare and standing as far away from the sharp teeth as she could.

"Yamayol," Eddie Marlowe said. "Your earthly kingdom is taken from you. Whether you can prevail at the end of the Liminal Year, I do not know, but it doesn't matter. You're playing a fool's game, which you cannot win."

"You may be Heaven's tool," Yamayol growled, straining his muscles beneath layers of rope and electric cable and duct tape, "but you cannot command me."

Eddie frowned. "Why not?"

"Because he has your soul!" Chuy blurted out.

Qayna moved her lips, but the sound that emerged was more like wind than words. Suddenly, Yamayol was no longer alone, but bound the earth with dozens—hundreds—thousands of human souls. They hung from his body like fruit, they were nailed to him like trophies, they were lashed to his belt.

And among them was a ghostly-looking, faded Eddie Marlowe. Ghost-Eddie, Eddie's soul, had more flesh on his bones than gaunt Living Eddie, but he had sadness in his eyes. Ghost-Eddie was clutched in Yamayol's hands, and the ropes binding Yamayol seemed to wind around him, too.

Eddie looked to Qayna, uncertain.

"Switch me for him," Chuy said. The words were heavy as they came from him, but Eddie and Qayna heard, and both looked in his direction.

"You cannot do that!" the Eagle cried. "Not in this world!"

Missy Broussard hissed and squirmed.

"Yes, I can," Qayna said. "It is an old truth, a bull for the high priest, a ram for Isaac. Chuy, are you really willing to do this?"

"Chuy …" Mike arrived, stumbling into the circle created by the mob. There were tears on his face.

"Mike," Chuy said. "Shut up, I'm doing this. Also, you should really think about the possibility that you might be gay. I'm not making fun of you, ese, I'm serious. It wouldn't matter to anyone else, but it might make you happier. Also … puta madre, I forgive you."

Mike fell to his knees, nodding and weeping. "I love you, brother."

Behind him came Sharon and the girls, who rushed to Eddie's side. Somehow, despite the fact that he was holding the banner, Eddie managed to wrap an arm around his entire family.

"I'm willing," Chuy said to Qayna. "Does it matter that I think I'm dying … ah, fading out of existence already?"

She shook her head. Then she spoke a few more words, made obscure gestures with both hands …

And his perspective changed. He was still fading, the edges of his vision beginning to tremble and dissipate like smoke on the breeze. He saw Missy Broussard, hovering above the Eagle and seething. Ghost-Eddie was gone.

Back where he belonged, probably.

"You're banished," Eddie said to Yamayol. "Both of you. You may never return to this land, or to molest these people."

"What do you think you're going to do?" Yamayol rumbled. "They'll all die, and then they'll be mine anyway."

"We will make a city here," Eddie said. "Not for the perfect, but for the willing. For those who will try. And when the time comes for the final battle, we will climb the staircase that you have built for us, and we will win the war."

Yamayol snarled, but said nothing.

"Thank you," Chuy said.

"Thank *you*," Eddie said. "This isn't over." Chuy's vision had shrunk to Eddie's face and a small halo of light around it. The clouds had cleared, or the light from the Ensign made Eddie appear to be made of gold.

"You think you can pull me out of Hell twice?" Chuy asked.

"I think we can get rid of Hell entirely," Eddie said.

Chuy stopped.

ALSO BY D. J. BUTLER

ABOUT THE AUTHOR

D.J. (Dave) Butler has been a lawyer, a consultant, an editor, a corporate trainer, and a registered investment banking representative. His novels have won the Whitney Award, the Association for Mormon Letters Award for Novel, and the Dragon Award. He plays guitar and banjo whenever he can, and likes to hang out in Utah with his wife, their children, and the family dog.

OTHER WORDFIRE PRESS TITLES BY D.J. BUTLER

Our list of other WordFire Press authors and titles is always growing. To find out more and shop our selection of titles, visit us at:

wordfirepress.com